WRITERS REPUBLIC

INNOCENT BUT GUILTY

WRITTEN BY
KENDRICK CRAFT

CREATIVE EDITOR
TONYA A. JOHNSON

WRITERS REPUBLIC L.L.C.
515 Summit Ave. Unit R1
Union City, NJ 07087, USA

Website: *www.writersrepublic.com*
Hotline: *1-877-656-6838*
Email: *info@writersrepublic.com*

Ordering Information:
Quantity sales. Special discounts are available on quantity purchases by corporations, associations, and others. For details, contact the publisher at the address above.

Library of Congress Control Number:		2021902498
ISBN-13:	978-1-63728-247-2	[Paperback Edition]
	978-1-63728-248-9	[Digital Edition]

Rev. date: 03/01/2021

PROLOGUE TITLE 1:21 A.M.

Fourteen years earlier, Daddy and I were cleaning his 1974 Chevy Impala. The year was 1984. I was only 9-years old at the time. My dad had a job as a woodsman and my mother was a stay-at-home mom. She kept this house neat. My two brothers always called mom a neat freak, because she would always tell them to clean their room. I had my own room. The house came from my great grandparents. It was passed down to my mom. This house was very old; a two-story townhome which sat at the end of the block in the circle of harmony.

Mom and Dad were from Kansas City. The two moved to this town after my mom's mother and father passed away. Then, my mom took over the house. Lance was the only child at the time. I believe Lance was 4 going on 5. That's the story I heard when we sat around the house for family story time. Lance always had the scariest stories to tell. One night, his story was so scary, I couldn't sleep. I slept with Mom and Dad for almost 2 days, trembling under the covers.

Lance told a story about a headless closet family that always came out when the clock struck 1:21 a.m. He said that the walls would get mildew on it. Veins would form on the walls to the ceiling. Just the thought of it would give me the creeps. Until one night I was awake in my bed and it was raining so hard that the wind pushed the tree branches against the window of my bedroom, it felt as if the house sway side to side, the roof creek and crack as if someone was walking on top of our house. I was holding my baby doll so tightly under my covers, everybody was asleep in the house and the clock sat right there on the nightstand, the glow in the dark numbers show the time was 1:17 a.m. then my little mind was thinking of the story Lance told. I can here

Lance saying how the headless family father used an axe to make his kill & take the head of his victim, to see where to go throughout the rest of the house I closed my eyes trying to get Lance's voice out of my conscience.

Once I opened my eyes, the rain had stopped but the wind was still strong. Strong enough to push the flutters back and forth against my window. My room smelled wet and darkness covered my room as if the moonlight was covered by the clouds. I could hear waterdrops, like in the scary movies, they made me want to jump from under my covers and run downstairs to mom and dad's room.

I began to count. My dad always told me when you count to ten your fears will no longer be there. So, I began to count one one thousand, two one thousand, three one thousand, four one thousand, five one thousand, six one thousand... And there was a creek; a creek so loud and lasted so long it sounded like my dad's tool shed door was opening in the backyard.

I started to count again seven one thousand, eight one thousand... hard footsteps filled my room, and I could fill someone standing beside my bed. My digital clock glowed in the dark reading 1:21a.m. and a shadow walked pass the clock and stood right in front of it.

I knew it, I knew someone was in my room. My dad's remedy didn't work, I said to myself, I was shaking out of my P. J.'s when my cover was pulled back with force. There it was...a headless man with a child who was reaching out at me. I screamed. I screamed so loudly that whoever was asleep woke up in the house.

My dad didn't come and neither did my mom. Lance or Bryant didn't come either. I was so scared that I jumped from my bed and ran towards the door stepping in a puddle of water. The carpet was drenched. My brother's room door was closed. I forced my way in as two people were picking up my brothers' heads off the floor and putting them onto their bodies.

When they turned around, they saw me. The two people looked like a big Lance and a big Bryant with my brothers' heads. They ran towards me, but I ran downstairs. Mom and Dad were sitting on the sofa. I yelled, "Mom, Dad! They are here! The headless family is here in the house!"

Rushing pass the sofa and noticing two bodies lying on the floor it was Mom and Dad. A little girl was on the sofa in between the two people whom I had mistaken for my mom and dad because they had stolen their heads off their bodies. I ran the opposite way towards the front door but slipped down on the wet carpet when I noticed it wasn't water but instead it was blood.

I could hear the two footsteps in the puddles as I was lying on my stomach on the carpet filled with blood. The first person grabbed me by my leg. I turned around and looked at the man who had my dad's head. I covered my face with both arms as if I could stop the big red axe from chopping my head off. My body went limp and my world was filled with total darkness.

THIS STORY WILL BE COMING SOON

INTRODUCTION

As I lay in my 3x8 foot one-man cell, peering from my jail issued blanket counting the bricks for almost one hundredth times, there was almost 705 bricks to be exact. In front of me were two square half-inches thick coated with plastic glass panels. It was maybe 4 am and I still cannot believe I let this happen to me. How could I let myself fall into a place like this? I remember when I was only 6 years old, a little boy, my cousin told me about this place and how bad this place could be.

He said one time he was doing his routine rounds and one of the inmates must have went hysterical on his watch and he noticed a man standing but dangling from the ceiling, as he called for backup, I was scared, as he told me that story. I was only 6 years old and he told me that this was not a place I would want to be, I could remember that story from almost 30 years ago.

But still shocked to be away from my family, away from my wife, away from my kids. What is going to happen to King, my Rottweiler. King only listens to my wife, my oldest son and myself. My oldest son was 21-years old away in college at the University of Texas. My daughter was back at home pregnant with her second child and my wife was self-employed running her independent insurance company. Her job met the bills but without me there, she's losing her mind, to know every night she rolls over and I'm not in the bed.

I remember one night not coming home from pulling an extra shift and she called my phone almost every half an hour until I told her I was pulling into the garage. But this was one of the most horrible times for her.

I am a contractor. I build skyscrapers. I remember when I received the call from Rudolph, my boss, who is a heavy built white man with red hair. He said I was one of his favorite contractors. I could weld almost anything together with my eyes closed and one hand behind my back, on one knee, with no gloves or a helmet...I was that good.

He called and said, "Get ready. We got the contract!" It was one to build a state-of-the-art bridge which was going to cut through town for almost 7-8 miles, connecting to another bridge that was almost 75 years old but somewhere at 3 miles the bridge was going to become higher than the Dallas, TX monument skyscraper. She was going to be higher than 80 stories for 2 miles in between the other mile and a half and this was to be done within two and a half years.

Well, being a contractor, you know it will take an extra 8 months because the city was doing more than one thing and our mayor and government dipped into the money a lot to fix and repair streets that citizens have been complaining about, law enforcement agencies may need more high-tech equipment, community programs for elderly citizens, so yes, an extension is always needed for high priority jobs like this one. That was music to my ears because for a minute I was beginning to get nervous since work was slow and hours were short now that the economy was at its turning point. Wall Street looked like it was going to have to pack up and file for unemployment soon.

When I rolled over, I saw my wife was sound asleep. She was so beautiful. I remember back in high school, she was the girlfriend of Ron, short for Ronelle. He was our high school quarterback and I played strong safety. Sometimes, coach would pull me up for a running play to help assist the strong safety when he took his tight end and moved him to the right. Nicole Harris, she was the lead cheerleader, about 5 feet 4 inches, sexy caramel, short black hair to her ear lobes, beautiful brown eyes and she had this nose ring. I remember standing in the hall for first period and seeing that she was so excited, "I got it!" She yelled to her girlfriends and how it hurt for almost that whole day, but she was Ron's girl. I really like Nicole, for graduation year, we all went off to different colleges except for me and Nicole, but our prom is when it happened.

I guess when she broke the news that she was going to LSU to Ronelle, he was pissed. So, pissed that he left her at the prom to have no ride home. Back then, I was a popular person myself, everybody at school knew me. I loved to rap in the hallway, or the boys' restroom, inside the gym, on the yard, you could not miss me. Nicole and her friends used to walk and stop to listen, and I knew the way she used to look at me that one day she was going to all mine.

CHAPTER

1

Twenty-four years later, Nicole Harris is now Nicole Tucker. We were married at age 23. She had our first son at 22 years old, and then our daughter was born a year later. Nicole finished high school and graduated from LSU with her bachelor's degree in Business. Architecture was always my thing. I used to get in my last period class and do a number with Lego blocks.

One year, our school had a science tournament and my class won first place. My classmates and I built a dump truck using Legos that was almost the size of the teacher's desk. I will never forget how Zeek, who was Asian, wired the truck with a few speaker wires and two big batteries that belonged to a power wheel and added the lights and a hydraulic kit to the bucket and gave it mobility and life to roll and for the bucket to raise up and down and tilt back and forward. That was one of the greatest projects the principal said when we presented our project at the auditorium.

Teachers came and rated our exhibit for first place, after we won the contest our project sat in the front office of the administration building for almost 3 weeks when someone broke the damn masterpiece to pieces. We were mad for almost 2 months, but anyway that was the days.

Now today, I'm building monuments for multi-billionaires, for companies like Chase America, Mal-Mart, Hewlett Packard and other big names but after my run in with the law, that kind of change things.

One night, coming from some friends, I saw a stalled vehicle on the highway flashers on, but with no one was standing on the side of the highway next to the vehicle as I passed by it. I was still listening to Anita Baker. Back when I was coming up, my mom used to 'love her some Anita' as she would put it.

She would play Anita Baker so loud coming up the sidewalk you could almost hear her from where the school bus would pick up and drop us off. I had two other siblings, an older brother and younger sister. Once my sister started being able to go to school with us, it was like walking an 80-year-old woman from one side of the house to the other side.

She would cry because her legs were tired, she would let her schoolwork fly in the wind. While I hold her, my brother will run and catch as much of the work he could. Man, that girl was a pain. My momma used to watch the three of us off to church when she was overworked in the house and would scream from the porch, "hold my baby's hand and watch for the cars," she would say. And she wanted us to tell Sister Scott that she's sorry she wasn't able to make it this Sunday. We would all scream, "Yes Ma'am." My sister was only 4 years old at the time. She would repeat what we said, and everything she hears she would repeat it too. My siblings are all grown up now; married with their own families.

The stalled vehicle was now in my rearview as I exited the highway. I looked down at my gas gauge and I realized I was gonna need gas. The gas station was just past the light to the right. The red light turns green as I crossed over the intersection of Hampton and pulled into Exxon to a pump. A lady and a little girl were at a pump but with no vehicle, only with a gas can in hand. The lady walked away, turned and told the little girl, who looked to be almost 12 years old, "Stay there Honey so no one can get the pump. Momma's going to be right back." The little girl waited like her mom told her. I got out of my vehicle and grabbed my ATM card from my wallet. I walked around to start my transaction, pushing in my zip code and after the pump authorized my card, I placed the nozzle into the gas hole after removing the gas cap and started to pump.

I began back around my car and got back into my Cadillac SUV. I kept an eye on the young girl to make sure no one kidnapped her or something of the sort because these days, there are crazy people in this world that would do a thing like that. They could be mad at the world figuring the world owes them something.

The little girl's mother returned to her; I was jamming to Anita Baker still. After getting into the groove of Anita Baker, singing 'The Best Thing Yet,' I laid my head back on the headrest and closed my eyes. I was feeling the next song smoothly coming through my speakers. The knock on the window scared me a little as the young lady and her young daughter stood on the other side. I turned down my music and rolled down my window.

She then said, "Sir, your gas is leaking out." "Oh Lord! Thanks!" I stated, as the lady and her child stepped back to let me out. I ran around my Escalade to see that my gas was all over the ground and I quickly removed the nozzle from my gas tank hole. I placed it back into its receiver, turned around and placed the cap back on my tank. I waited for my receipt and rushed back around to get on home because I knew my wife would be worried sick about me wondering where I was.

At that point, I looked up and noticed the lady and her daughter was still standing on the side of my truck. I thanked her and then she asked, "Sir if it wouldn't be a problem, could you please help us back to our vehicle back up the highway?" She explained that her "daughter has to be to school early in the morning plus I have this 15-gallon gas can filled with almost $30.00 of gas. It's too heavy for the both of us. I can pay you."

I thought for a second about the one hundred million things my wife was going to worry about and then come looking for me and notice our truck at the gas station. What if the woman staged the whole "out of gas" scene to get me robbed? What if I did take her and she told someone that I raped her or whatever after I left? What if the car does not start, then I would hear 'could I take her home'? So, after all of the 'what if thinking,' I decided to be a great gentleman, and told the woman sure hop on in."

I thought to myself, Tyrone Tucker what have you done? Do you know who your wife is? Private eye, Nicole. Man, you are not going to hear the end of this. She's going to start off by saying, "It's late. Where have you been? I can smell perfume all over you. I called Troy and he said you had left an hour ago. Don't you lie to me, Tyrone Tucker. Yada! Yada! Yada!"

Man, my wife can be such a mouth, but I love her. I love my wife for many, many reasons. I never stepped out of my marriage for the 23 years we've been together. The young mother and her daughter hopped in and I suddenly remembered she held a gas can in her lap. Then, I told her I could put the gas can behind the 3rd row seat. Immediately, my truck was filled with the fragrance of unleaded gas. I thought to myself gosh this is some stinky stuff.

The lady handed the can full of gas to me and I rushed it off like a stinky baby's pamper to the backyard garbage can. As I opened the back door to my SUV and placed the gas can on the side of my custom-made sound system. I had a professionally installed subwoofer box made by Kickers, which was made out of Plexiglas; two 1,500-watt amps, one 1,700-watt amp and a filtered replica for my E.Q. I was really nervous to have to place this can of gas back there with almost $6,000.00 worth of sound system equipment, but being a gentleman, I felt like I'll get my blessings. "Thank you, Jesus," as my wife would put it. I closed the door but opened it right back up to place a heavy quilt over the can to prevent some of the aroma that filled the truck atmosphere with such a horrible stench. I closed the door and walked back to the driver's seat, got in and fastened my seat belt. I rolled the windows down just a crack so we would not suffocate from the gas fumes from the can. I had been told too many times that gas, plus in my profession I already know if you breath too much gas, can cause your lungs to collapse.

As I began to pull off, the lady had complimented my truck and said, "This is a nice truck," while strapping her seat belt on and reaching back to tell her daughter to do the same. She introduced herself by saying, "My name was Charity Hunter, and this is my daughter, Rene Hunter. I'm sorry." Then, I told her, "My name is Tyrone Tucker." "Okay," she said giving comfort amongst each other, but I still went with thought number one million and four that she can be lying.

As Charity repeated, "This is a nice truck." I reached back and replied, "Thank you." I try keeping it that way. I got caught at the red light. My thoughts went back to my wife, pulling up on side of us saying, "Who's that? Pull over. Get out of my truck Winch. Yeah. That's who you be creeping with…She's ugly! Yada! Yada! Yada!"

As I smiled from the thought, Charity started to tell me where her vehicle was, and I told to her. "You know, I saw your vehicle on the side of the road." Charity said, "You did?" I replied, "Yes. I was going to stop but I didn't see anyone. So, I kept going. Then, I realized I needed gas and there you two were at the pump." Charity said, "What a coincidence, because I really thought Rene and I were going to have to hike all the way back there." I told her, "Well, that is a long walk." She thanked me again.

It got quiet for a second. My name tag was hanging around my rearview mirror and was dangling out of control from the wind coming through the window. My wife's picture rested on the dashboard and Charity noticed the beautiful smiling woman, and asked, "Your wife?" I looked over with a big smile on my face, "Yes," I answered. "She's a lucky woman," she replied.

I knew from that point, Charity was flirting, and she kept going. She said, "I don't see a ring." So, I rolled my hand over and showed her my ring. It was a sterling silver wedding band with almost 30 crushed diamonds across the top. "My wife picked it out last year for our 22nd year anniversary." Charity exploded, "22 years!" I said, "Actually it's 23 years being married but we spent 4 years of college dating. So, 27 years altogether." Charity said, "Almost 30 years huh?" "Yep," I stated. Charity began by saying Rene's father didn't last long. She's 13 years old now. He left us when she was almost 3 years old.

He's a dead beat like the rest of them. I asked did she have any other kids and Charity replied quickly, "Oh no! That's my only one." She said and last one, realizing we were pulling up to her vehicle. As I pulled behind it, she asked if I could pour the gas in the tank for her. I did not see any problem with that besides, she was a lady, and it would not be right to sit in the truck and watch her struggle lifting it to the tank.

So, I got out of the truck, walked to the back, opened the door, removed the quilt from over the can and lifted it up and out. I closed the door and walked over to the stalled vehicle to begin administering the gas after removing the cap. In about 5 to 7 minutes, all the gas was in her vehicle and she stepped out for the first time. I noticed that Charity was shorter than myself. I was 5 ft. 9' tall so, she had to be almost 5 ft. 2 or something of the sort. Maybe a little shorter than my wife.

As she reached in from the passenger side of her vehicle with her keys in hand and cranked up her car, she had a Toyota Camry seem to be a newer model from the previous year. She reached back and got out of the car, waved her daughter to come on and asked me, "How much I owe you?" Again, Tyrone being a gentleman, I said, "Oh nothing." She said, "You sure. I can afford to give you $10.00?"

I thought to myself...$10.00...Ha! I cannot do anything with $10.00 besides, she may need it to grab a bite to eat for herself and her daughter, I told her, "That's ok you keep it." She asked her daughter to sit in the car and close the door. "How about lunch one day or dinner?" She said she knows how to cook and that her mom was from Louisiana.

I knew Louisianans know how to get down in the kitchen. I thought my wife could cook herself. So, I told her, "Nah. I don't want to get anything started and love to keep things the way they were but thank you." As I walked off, Charity said, "Thank you, Tyrone." I turned around and said, "You're welcome." and watched Charity get in her vehicle and put her left blinker on and took out into the night. I, then, did the same. I realized she took the same exit I usually take when she went left. So, I went right.

I sat at the red light looking at the same time. It was now 15 minutes to midnight, and I'm surprised my wife hadn't called to ask that million-woman survey questionnaire. You know that questionnaire your wife has, and it starts with "What are you doing? Where you at? Where you been? Do you know what time it is? Why are you getting in so late? What is keeping you so long? Why you never called? Yada, Yada, Yada."

Then, finally my phone rings. It's Nicole... "Hey Honey. I know it's late, Baby." I said giving her a chance to speak. "I was over at Troy's and the fellas. You know that" I said. I told her, "I'm sorry, Baby. I must have lost track of the time. I'm on my way home now." She told me before we hung up that I need to stop and get something to eat. That is her way of letting me know she did not fix me a plate or put one up for me. "She's mad," I said to myself.

I pulled up into the driveway and opened the garage. We had a two-car garage. I remember at one time, it was full of boxes, old furniture, winter clothes, my tools, her exercise equipment, bikes, ladders, all kinds of power tools, etcetera. But ever since I built that shed in the back, a lot of our belongings went there, most to a garage sale all of her older stuff she didn't want anymore. And, we had a donation charity to the old folks' home last Christmas. You should have seen some of those folks faces.

You know the saying your old junk is another person's treasure, well & true and those people were so happy. Not only did my wife give her belongings, but she also cooked dinner and fed the whole place. The people were so grateful that year, my wife planned on repeating that again this year. I pulled into my garage and let it down. Then, walked into the house.

We had a one-story flat with 5 bedrooms and 1 guest room. The other room was made into an office for my wife. She worked from home and bringing in some good business. She was the person who placed insurance on companies that started fresh in the business world, and man I tell you she stays swamped with clients. She has been talking about leasing a building for her busy line of work, and actually hire agents to set up different accounts.

The alarm beeps as I put in the code to turn it off and re-entered the code to set stay. My daughter was back home because she was not doing too well on her own then and pregnant again. My daughter was only 20 years old and pregnant with her second child. My wife is probably in the bed waiting on me so she could go to sleep. I walked to the back door. King was tall enough to stand on his back legs and look through the backyard door window I spoke thru the glass what's up big man.

I raised King since he was a little pup now, he's a giant of a dog he began scratching at the window crying like a big baby just happy to see me I'm probably the only person in the house he saw today my wife be busy, my daughter is still scared of him I turned to walk away he began to bark very loudly like he was asking 'where are you going?' He does it all the time.

The house still smelled of roast and gravy, and as it filled the house, I began to feel really hungry from all the beer. So, when I opened the refrigerator doors to pull out pots and began to close the door, there she was standing on the other side of the of the fridge door. She almost scared the black off me. "Hi Baby," I told her. She had this look on her face like, "Don't 'Hi Baby' me."

I began to explain the reason I was late getting in and she said, "I know! I know! You told me already." She says, "Ew, you stink of gas." I wanted to tell her the truth, but I told her that my tank had overfilled with gas and it spilled all over me. "Not paying attention?" She asked. She told me to move; get out her pots. Something my mom would say when I was a teenager. Then, Nicole started to say, "You need not get in the bed smelling like gas. Go take a shower. I'll fix your plate."

I walked past her and as I gave her a kiss, she started fanning the smell like it was smoky in the kitchen. "Thank you, Baby," and I walked towards the room. I passed up my daughter's room and peered through the doors. Both she and my granddaughter were sound asleep. My granddaughter was only 2 years old. We call her Diva because when she gets dressed up, all of a sudden something about her little walk because it changes as she begins to sway her little head from side to side. I told my daughter about letting her watch all those videos on B.E.T. It is starting to rub off on her.

As I continued walking down the hallway, I can still hear my wife in the kitchen fussing while slamming tops on pots and sliding plates across the countertops, I just smiled. My son's bedroom door has a padlock on it as if he is hiding something in there.

It had been that way for almost 3 years until he comes home on his school breaks. I passed by the guest room, the office and then our room. I walked straight to the restroom because I had been needing to empty my beer-filled bladder for a long time. The phone vibrated in my pocket; the clock that sat on the wall of the bathroom read 12:27 a.m. I figured it was Troy trying to see if I made it home safely. But the number showed private and I pressed Answer.

"Hello," I spoke. A soft voice said, "Can I speak to Tyrone?" I kind of wet the toilet seat because the voice sounded familiar. I said, "Speaking." "Hey. This is Charity." My heart skipped a beat as I looked at the bathroom door, looking for my wife to be standing there ready to ask, "Who's that you talking to?" But she was not there. I walked to the door, looked out and listened really hard for my wife to see if she was still in the kitchen.

I softened up my voice with a whisper, "how you get my number?" She laughed, I began to think and wondered when I got out of my truck at the gas station. My phone was on the charger. Did she get it then? I said, "No!" to myself because if that was so, then I would have seen the screen light still on. It was set for 5 minutes to stay on, and besides, I was not out the truck long enough.

Then, I thought about it, when she asked if I would pour her gas into her tank, I was out the truck a while. That is when she got it. I started telling her, "You can't be calling my phone. My wife is here." She stated telling me how much she wanted me, and how she just can't keep the smell of my truck out of her mind…How the Anita Baker song reminded her of how it could be with me and her sharing love with each other…how she wished she was my wife for 30 years with the same man. She went on to say, "Your wife must be satisfied," and she wanted to find out.

I could hear my wife coming down the hallway to the room. I hung up and turned on the tub water, nervously turning my phone off for the night. My wife asked, "You're taking a bath and not a shower Tyrone?" As she walked to the door and saw the urine on the toilet seat, she started to fuss about me not raising the toilet seat up. So, I wiped the seat clean of specimen and she got out the Lysol spraying disinfectant on the seat.

She told me your food is on the nightstand and my phone gave a buzz to let me know it was shutting down and Nicole looked and asked, "What's wrong with ya phone?" I pulled it out my pocket and said "Oh! It's dead." She paid no mind to what I said and began to say your food is getting cold. I took off all my clothes to my boxer shorts, undershirt and socks, emptied my pockets and placed my clothes into the dirty bend.

Then, I sat on my side of the bed and blessed my food. I began to dig in as gravy dripped down my fingers from picking up the roast. Licking my fingers clean of gravy, the dinner rolls were golden brown on top, mashed potatoes were very rich and buttery, and the string beans were full of garlic bacon pieces. I turned to see my wife smiling as she sat on the bed watching me as I dug through my plate. My wife loves to see me eat her cooking.

I was drinking a tall glass of icy Minute Maid Fruit Punch behind the great meal. Grabbing another slice of roast, repeating that same routine over again until that plate was empty. Nicole asked if I wanted more and for a moment, I was gonna say yes, but remembered it was almost one o'clock in the morning and I had not showered yet. Plus, my wife was nearly passed out, but she was trying her best to stay awake. Her eyes were turning red which made them look brownish burgundy.

I reached for my plate on the nightstand, walked around the bed to place the plate on the entertainment center dresser. Then, I grabbed my robe out of the closet. If my daughter wasn't home, I would have gone into the kitchen with my boxers on.

As I slipped on my robe and grabbed my plate, I headed into the kitchen, finishing off the icy cold Fruit Punch Minute Maid. I rinsed my plate and fork and pulled open the stainless-steel dishwasher. My kitchen was color coordinated with silver and black appliances and the countertop looked as though it was spotted with silver square pieces of black hardwood. My cabinets were black with silver knobs that stretched around the kitchen, with the touch of color from my wife, a deep-dish sink one sway handle that maneuvers from cold to hot water. My kitchen floor was made of all black marble tile.

As I began to wipe the sink free of water splashes, I could see King while standing in the window. He was at the back door looking at me with this "what you are doing" look in his eyes. I walked out the kitchen into the living area through the hall passed my daughter and my son's rooms, turned past the office, pass the guest room, into my room. My wife was asleep just like that.

I went straight to the shower and I washed up for 10 minutes. I turned off the water, grabbed for a dry towel and began to think about the lady I picked up to help at the gas station and how she snooped through my phone to call me. Plus, I thought...if she did that, I wonder if she could have followed me home. I was not able to remember if a car turned on my block to follow me. Hoping she did not do a dumb thing like that, I finished up drying off.

I sprayed the shower down with shower cleaner. We had a tub and a shower. My wife really used our deep mold tub because she loved sitting in the deep country porcelain tub Jacuzzi. That tub feels so good when it is full of hot water & skin soother. Once I had cleaned the shower thoroughly, I went to bed.

CHAPTER

2

Morning came very quickly as the sun poured through my bedroom, my grandchild was running through the hallway, Saturday was the day the landscapers would come I can hear weed eaters on side of the house. Then, I thought about King. He was a German Rock Wilder mixed with Shepherd. He was a huge dog, very strong and powerful. I raised up to realize Nicole was not in the bed this morning. Most Saturdays, she will still be in the bed.

And, then it hit me…Bacon gave a pleasant aroma throughout the house. Diva was playing in the hall. I called her and she came running in the hall towards my room. "Paw-Paw! Paw-Paw!" she exclaimed as she came in and climbed up into my bed. I said, "Why are you running in the hallway with all the noise?"

"I love you Paw-Paw," she said and gave me a little hug. "Paw-Paw loves you too, but why are you running in the hallway with all that noise?" I asked her again. She pointed to the hallway. I said to her, "Yeah. Why are you making all that noise? You woke Paw-Paw up."

She jumped from my grasp and crawled back out the bed and out into the hallway again. When Trenice came in my room, Daddy I need $60 to get my medication and I think Momma is calling you to come get King. "I'm getting up and I will see. When Trenice left out the room, I sat up, slipped out of the bed, closed the room door and put my shorts on with a pair of sandals. I went into the bathroom to wash my face and brush my teeth. Then, I headed into the kitchen with $60.00 in my hand.

My wife was sitting at table looking into the backyard, watching King standing by the gate barking at the landscapers. My wife said, "You need to go get his crazy butt. Look at him." Nicole said, "He is just wild. You really need to go get him." I walked out the door, "King!" I called out. He came running towards me like a happy kid but turned right back around to go check on the landscapers.

"Come here, King!" King came back. I snapped the chain that was on the ground to his collar. Then, I opened the gate to let the landscapers inside the backyard. King began barking at them. The dog was huge. I rolled the heavy chain around my hand to leave no slack, walked out front to the garage and pressed the code into the dial pad on the door.

The garage raised up and I put him inside the garage. I said, "Go sit down, King!" He went to sit down, and I closed the door back down. I went back into the yard, back into the kitchen and had breakfast with my wife. She was done so she got up and said that she was getting ready to leave to take Trenice to the pharmacy.

"Oh Baby!" Nicole said. "What's wrong? I just put King in the garage," I said. Nicole responded, "You know I hate when you put him in there. He scratched the Lexus last time and dented the garage door a little. I wanted to tell you that about him. You really need to do something with his big self."

I said to her, "Let them finish in the yard before you leave so I can put him back in the yard." Nicole asked, "What did he eat?" I said, "Nobody yet," Nicole smiled and said, "You are right. He is big enough to eat a human."

The landscapers finished about 30 minutes later on the backyard and I was in our bedroom when I heard the doorbell ring. I grabbed $75.00 and took it to the door. The guys do a real good job every weekend on my yard. I opened the door and handed the $75.00 to the young man. I thanked him and closed the door.

Then, I went, got King and let him in the house. King came strutting through the hallway. Diva had always been afraid of King, so she ran back into the room screaming. "King!" I yelled. "Go back to the kitchen." King went to the kitchen a little agitated from Diva screaming too loud and Trenice closed her bedroom door. I walked past the door and King peeped passed the kitchen wall to see if I was coming and ran back by the door. I remember when I first brought King to this house.

He was just a puppy. My wife loved that puppy. She used to take him everywhere she went. A lot of neighbors wanted him. One time, King somehow got out of the yard and was wandering the neighborhood when one of my wife's friends in the neighborhood called her and told her she thinks King had gotten out the yard.

She could recognize King from anywhere. He was 5 months at the time when he was roaming the neighborhood. At 5 months, he was big to be a puppy. His black coat with golden patches were unique in colors. He looked like a stuffed animal from a state fair booth. Nicole called me that day and told me that King had gotten out of the yard some kind of way. I was almost 40 stories in the air when she called. I was welding T-frames on a skyscraper. I called down to the foreman and told him I had an emergency at home that needed my attention.

Then, I called the crane operator to let him know that I was coming down on the west side of the building. The crane cable was attached to this mild steel homemade elevator we built for temporary use. This is actually where the elevator was to be placed after we put in the framing of the building. As I came down the crane moving very slowly, agitated from knowing that my awfully expensive dog was roaming the neighborhood, a lot of things crossed my mind that could happen to him. He could get hit by a car. He could scare off some people and he is just of puppy of 5 months. I made it to my truck.

At that time, I had an F-150. I got into my truck and must have done 90 mph all the way home, as if my child was left outside in the rain. When I pulled up to my street, I really did not know where to look and I rode around for a while until I saw King at the tree looking up barking. As I pulled up, I noticed something in the tree. It was a squirrel.

As King ran around the tree jumping as if he can get the rodent; shifting back and forth like he was trying to push that big oak tree down. The tree would not budge. I got out of the truck and called out to him. King looked at me and ran to me like a little kid. I opened the back bed of the truck and King hopped in the back. His little nubby tail was swaying side to side very fast as if he was happy to see me. I opened the yard door and King ran out into the yard.

I picked up his big giant dog bowl and poured 5 cups of dog food inside. It takes a lot to keep him full now that King is 4 years old. My wife came out then. King was more attached to her than he was to any of us. She used to have him more when he was a puppy. King ran to Nicole as soon as she stepped out in the yard to kiss me to let me know she was on her way out to the pharmacy with Trenice. She said they were going to make a few more runs before she would make it back and asked if I needed for her to pick up a few items for me.

I told her to check the post office box as she walked back waving King back; get away King. He looked as if he was smiling at her and ran back to his bowl of food. I went back into the house, closed the door, and in the room. I turned my phone back on. It was sitting on the nightstand on the charger. I walked to the closet to pick out something to put on for the day.

It is Saturday. The fellas are going to the bowling alley this evening and wanted me to join them. I pulled out a polo collared shirt with short sleeves with a pair of blue jean shorts and found my sandals Nicole bought for my birthday.

Nicole and I always buy each other things. Just last week my wife was showing me a blouse she wanted to buy herself and did not have the money. When we got home the next day, I went to that same store and purchased that same blouse that she wanted and laid it across the bed. Nicole came in from running daily chores that day and noticed it on the bed and Man my "in return" gift was better than the blouse I bought for her.

As I was laying out my clothes for the day, my cell began to ring more like vibrate on the nightstand, a private call. My first thought was it was the crazy woman from last night calling me back to curse me out for turning off my cell phone and hanging up on her. She's probably gonna threaten me about corning to my house and lie to my wife that me and her had an affair which would not be true, but who knows people these days would do anything.

Then, I thought maybe it's an important phone call that needed to be answered. So, I scanned the hallway, phone in hand looked and listened for the garage. I pressed talk, "Hello!" She was on the other end. "Hey Mr. Tyrone. Why are you acting like you're shy?" I threaten her about calling the cops, "This is harassment you know. And, plus you have invaded my privacy by snooping around in my phone. Now, if this continues," I carried on, "I will have you looked up and arrested."

Charity started speaking, "You would do that to a sweet little woman like myself?" In my mind, I was like "hell yeah". She continued, "I know where you live, and work. I will come to your house and meet your wife." As she continued with a question, "Isn't your wife's name Nicole Tucker, and your daughter is Trenice Tucker? You live at..."

My whole world came rushing into me when she called out my address. She told me about King, the landscapers and what I had on this morning. She said she even saw when my wife left in the navy-blue Lexus." Charity continued, "Your wife is going into Mal-Mart now. How about I go and speak with her and meet my new step-daughter."

At this point, I lost my cool and I shouted, "Listen you crazy psycho ass woman. I don't know why you're doing this." Click. Charity hung up. "Hello!" I blurted "Damn!" I hurried up and put my clothes on, rushed to the truck, opened the garage and pulled out to head to Mal-Mart to catch up with Nicole and Trenice.

Remembering that I did not set the alarm on the house but that could wait; she's in the same facility with Nicole, my grandchild and daughter. Who knows what she can pull off after telling me all my information?

Mal-Mart was pretty swamped, and the parking lot was looking overcrowded. Nicole and Trenice walked down the aisle pushing a cart with little Diva in the seat part of the cart. As Nicole picked out items, Trenice was talking to her daughter as a woman walked up. "Mrs. Tucker!" Nicole turned around and Diva and Trenice looked at the strange woman who waved.

"Hi! My name is Charity!" "Ok!" Nicole said in suspense. "Well, I know you don't know me, but do you still offer insurance for new companies?" Nicole smiled, "Yes." Nicole answered very politely. Nicole asked Charity, "Ms. or Mrs.?" "No. I'm not married," Charity answered. "Well Ms. Charity. Have you seen my commercials or an ad in the business section?"

Charity replied, "Yes." "Can I get a business card?" Charity asked. Nicole reached into her purse and came out with a business card. Handed it to Charity. "Well, I don't want to hold you up Mrs. Tucker. We will talk on a business account soon. Let's say Monday morning." Nicole agreed, "Great. Monday would be fine." Charity and Nicole shook hands and Charity was getting ready to pass Trenice and Diva when she stopped and said to Diva "you're a cutie".

Trenice smiled and told Diva to say thank you. Diva said in a little voice, "Thank you." Charity told Trenice "Girl, I remember when I was walking in your shoes. I know how you feel." The three ladies kind of smirked as she told Trenice "Ice cream. Plenty of it," and walked off. "She was nice," Nicole said. They finished shopping. Tyrone called Nicole's phone to see where she was in the store. Nicole picked up, "Hey Honey." "Hey baby," I followed, "'where are you?'" "In Mal-Mart," Nicole answered. "I know that. Where at in Mal-Mart?" Tyrone asked.

"At the pharmacy now. We are just getting to it," Nicole began to say. "Hello," she realized that Tyrone hung up. "That was your father. He's here at Mal-Mart." "Daddy at Mal-Mart?" Trenice said. "Daddy doesn't even like coming here." Nicole finished by saying, "What man likes coming to Mal-Mart?" Trenice looked at her belly. Nicole said, "Never mind making a joke about her daughter's pregnancy because this is where Trenice met her second baby's father at.

Diva yelled, "Paw-Paw!" Tyrone came walking up. "Hey ladies," I called out. Trenice said, "Daddy, what are you doing here?" Nicole says, "Yeah. What are you doing here?" "I thought you don't like Mal-Mart!" "Well, I only don't like it when it's crowded." Trenice and Nicole looked around at the crowd, "Yeah. I know." Tyrone said, "It's crowded. I figured since I'm here I might as well come on in now." "'Okay again Tyrone Tucker."

"What are you here to get that you couldn't call me to tell me to get?" Tyrone thought for a second, "A case of beer for the fellas. That's what I came for." "Beer?" Nicole said, "You and the other beer heads with all this drinking. Didn't you drink last night?" "Yeah." Tyrone answered. "So, again today?" Nicole asked.

Tyrone began by saying, "That's not all I came here for. I figured you might need some more money, and King needs some more dog food. He's getting low." Nicole said "Money! Tyrone are you offering me money I thought you said." Tyrone looked around, "Forget about what I said. Baby, I just figured you might need more money and from the looks of it, looking down into the basket, you just may need more money." "Tyrone, I don't need any more of your money, and King doesn't need any more dog food. I just bought another 50-pound bag of that stinky stuff. It's in the garage.

If you slow down, maybe you would have seen it. Boy you make me wonder sometimes," Nicole carried on and on. "Now, if you are here for your beer. It's by the water aisle." "Okay Honey," Tyrone replied and then reached to kiss his wife and wave off Diva and Trenice. He, then, walked off to get the case.

Tyrone was checking out and saw a friend of the family coming in as he was leaving out. "Hey Tyrone. How's it coming," a couple walked up to him. It was the Washington's...Perry and Sandra Washington. They stayed in our neighborhood. "What you got there neighbor?" Perry said as he turned to his wife and said, "See Sandra I told you that was Tyrone Tucker." Tyrone stated, "Aww man going to catch the bowling alley with a few buddies." "Oh yeah. You look like you guys are going to have fun." Perry said, "Aw Man. You know how we fellas do it."

Sandra asked me "How's Nicole?" "She's fine, as a matter of fact, she's here in Mal-Mart now. Her, Trenice and my grandbaby." Sandra asked, "How's her pregnancy coming along?" I started by saying, "She's fine. Nicole is like her pregnancy coach. They were back at the pharmacist last time I saw them." Hey, I cut the conversation short and told them nice seeing you two...okay. Bye.

They walked off and I walked off. I got to my truck and noticed a letter on my windshield wiper. I opened the truck's back door, dropped the case on the floor, closed the door, peeled the letter out from under the windshield wipers, got into the truck and opened it up. It said, "Hey Tyrone. This is Charity. I met your wife. She is a sweet woman. You have a beautiful family. Your grandbaby is adorable. Can't wait to see what the inside of your home looks like. Love always, Charity... Smooches Baby."

I began to ball up the letter as a knock on my window scared me. It was Nicole. "Hey! Help me put the groceries in the car, Honey." I quickly dropped the letter on the floor and got out the truck locked it and walked about 4 car aisles over to my wife's car. She asked, "What were you reading dear?" "Oh, a flier someone put on my windshield."

"Don't you hate that?" Nicole asked, "I wish I could catch them putting the fliers out so I could tell them to stop putting those papers on my car," I was still putting bags in the trunk while Trenice grabbed Diva and placed her inside her car seat. I finished putting the bags in the trunk and closed it. My wife hugged me and said, "Thanks you hunk of a man." Then, she kissed me. I told her, "I love you Honey." Then, reached over and opened her door.

She got in and I closed the door. Nicole started up the car and rolled down the window and asked if I was coming home. I told her maybe a little later Nicole said, "I'm gonna drop off these groceries and pass by my momma's to see how she is doing." Last week my mother-in-law took sick and had to go to the hospital. The doctor said it was something she ate. Apparently, my mother-in-law was not properly eating. So, the doctor told Nicole to watch her eating habits.

I said, "See you later, Baby," and I watched as my wife backed out of that parking spot. At that moment, I remembered that I was the one who taught her how to drive. Man, that was the most horrific time of my life. We also had a Toyota Camry back before her Lexus. Man, I tell you, Nicole did a number on that car paint. I tell you she ran up against the tree at the house, scratched the driver's side from the blinker light to the taillight. I spent $600.00 getting that car repaired.

Then, one day she was trying to parallel park and Man she slammed into another car in the parking lot. That lady was so mad at Nicole that her blood pressure ran up. She had a pearl white Q45 Infiniti that looked to be brand new. The insurance company paid the damages on both vehicles but threaten that if Mrs. Tucker did not get her driving skills together, they were going to take her off the insurance policy.

So, one night, I know I spent 3 hours in an empty parking lot teaching her how to parallel park. She finally got it and now she tries telling me how to drive. I just can't wait until Trenice starts driving on her own. I said I was going let her start at a driving academy to take the headache away from me, of showing her how to drive.

When I made it back to the truck, my cell phone rung. I pressed talk without scanning my phone I.D saying "Hello." "Hey Tyrone." I started, "Charity you really need to stop doing this, for real. You are going to get me in a jam with my marriage lady. Do you even care about someone's vows?" "If you give me what I want," she started, "I'll leave you alone. I promise. I will leave you alone forever. I'll erase your number and cancel the meeting Monday at 11:30 a.m. that I have with your wife, Nicole." I began to think, and she continued, "Did you get my letter?" I replied, "Yes. I got your letter." "Good! Hey! Why don't you and I meet up this evening and talk about this? Let's say China Wok. I love Chinese food," she said.

"Okay I agreed." "Great! You know which one?" I began thinking of the city where all the China Woks I only knew of four of them. There was one up the street from here, 2 on the east side of town which would be a great place since it's so far out and one on Main street which is 2 miles away from my house. And before I could say which one Charity said, "Let's meet at the China Wok on Main Street, if that's not too far out your way." Dammit, I thought she read my mind, "See you let's say about 8 o'clock," I started to ask, "Why so late?" She told me she had her reasons.

I really did not trust this woman. How do I know she will live up to her word? And I just wanted this to be final, "8 O'clock it is." "Come dressed to impress Mr. Tucker." She hung up. I wanted to call the cops and tell them everything. Tell them where we were going to meet up and have her arrested. What if she is expecting me to do a thing like that and have someone to harm my family? She knows where I live, she met my wife, my daughter, not only that, but my grandbaby too. She was a case.

You do not just try to bring to trial and convict her just off what she says. I will have to get something recorded. She is calling me private. That won't stand up in court how would they know if it was her? How would they be able to say Charity Hunter was harassing me and she beat the case in court. Then, send some of her psycho friends to hurt my wife and my family. Hell, with that thought I made up my mind not let her harm my family. I'll just cooperate but someone has to know about this. "Troy," I said out loud. I will tell Troy tonight when we meet up at the bowling alley.

CHAPTER

3

I rode around for a while before I decided to phone Troy and find out where they were. It was now 4 pm Saturday evening I have a case of Bud Light beer for the fellas and ready to take it to them. Back in college Troy and I used to team up on the bowling lanes and destroy our competition when we walked away, we would leave the score card with almost eleven strikes. Each ending between the both of us. We became the talk of the lane when Troy and I came in. Man, you can hear the alley say, "Oh shit. It's Troy and Tyrone.

Those two guys are a great team." I can remember back in college there was this team called the Power Bowlers and Man, I tell you it was four of them. They were all great but one of their men used to be on fire. I mean every bowler had their own personal bowling ball. At that time, Nicole was pregnant with Tyrone Jr. She used to say "Are y'all going to beat them with just two of you, Baby?" Two-man T-Man…That's when we got our name because between a four-man team; just us two men.

Troy must have gotten STRIKES 8 times in a row and I came right behind him. Those guys were so totally off their game once they saw the two of us in action. The college recorded the tournament the next day. The newspaper around campus was bragging so much about the two of us that the bowling alley made two shirts that had our last names on it Tucker # 1, Sage #2 and until this day those shirts are in a frame over the bar in the bowling alley.

Troy finally picked up the phone and said, "Talk fast. I'm getting dressed." "Hey! What time are we getting up there?" I'm here. Brent and Leon up there already, "Well, I'm out and about myself," Troy said. "I have something I need to talk to you about." Troy said, "Hit me with it once I get up to the lane." "Cool!" I said and hung up.

I called my wife, Nicole, to see if she was still at her mom's house. When she picked up the phone, she said, "Hey Baby." "Hi Honey!" I returned. "How are you?" Nicole said fine. So, I asked, "How's your mom?" "She's doing okay," Nicole said. "I'm still here warming her up some soup. I've rolled her hair up and put lotion on her legs. Tyrone, she asked how your work is coming alone." "Let me speak with her." I could hear Nicole in the kitchen. She came back to the phone, "Hold on Sweetie. She is in the back. Let me walk back to her." I quickly asked, "Is she in the bed?" "Yes, she's in the bed." Nicole said.

"Oh, okay." I could hear Nicole walking into her mom's room. I could also hear the television, then Nicole said, "It's Tyrone..." Letting her mom know it's me on the phone. My mother-in-law's voice came across the phone. Her voice sounded so tired and she was such a sweet lady, "Hey Tyrone," she slowly spoke.

"Hey Momma, are you feeling better?" I asked as I pulled up to the bowling lane. She asked me what I said, I repeated, "Are you feeling better Momma? Are you okay?" "Yes, Tyrone. I'm okay. Why haven't you come to see me?" I really did not have anything to answer back with on that question. "I'm sorry Momma. I was hanging out last night and today. I'm at the bowling alley now. I'm sorry Momma. I'm going to pass through later when I leave here and come tuck you in, okay Momma, before I go home."

Momma began to say, "Well you know Nicole here and she rolled up my hair. It looks really nice. You ought to see it Tyrone. It is beautiful. She's making me some soup now." "That's great momma," I said. "When did you say you were gonna come over?" My mother-in-law asked. "I'll be there before I head home tonight." "Okay Son. I'll be looking forward to seeing you," she continued to talk, "I'm thankful for Nicole. She's my little angel you know."

I started by saying, "Yes Ma'am." She continued, "Out of the rest of my children, Nicole always did the right thing." As I waved my hand, impatiently in a rush to get to this case of beer, I got the fellas flagging me to get out of the truck. From the corner of my eyes, I can see Troy pulling into the parking lot; looks to have a passenger. And my mother-in-law was still going, "Hey remember that time," she continued as Troy, Leon and Brent was walking over to the truck, I gave them the 'one second' finger. They seemed to get impatient waving me off as they walked towards the lane.

My thoughts began to soar when I was a teenager, Mrs. Harris used to drop Nicole off in front of the high school and say pick you up after school. She would watch Nicole off until one day Mrs. Harris was accompanied by her husband, Nicole's father, Mr. Harris. He was, to my understanding, a bricklayer. He looks to be picking up on concrete all day in the blazing sun; he was ruff. He let Nicole and her 2nd to the oldest sister out of the car.

I noticed Ronelle and his boys were standing in front of the school. He walked over to Nicole as she was coming towards the podium and he threw his arm around Nicole. Man, Nicole's dad got out of that car and walked over to Ronelle grabbed him by his arm and picked him up into the air. At first, we all thought Mr. Harris was going to slam him on the ground on top of his head, but he didn't.

Mr. Harris told Ronelle while he was dangling in the air, next time I catch you with your cruddy arm or hands on my daughter, I'm going to slam you on your head. Nicole was pleading with her dad to leave him alone and so was Mrs. Harris. Mr. Harris was like James Evans from Good Times. Man, since that day, Ronelle would wait until he saw Nicole's parents leave out of sight before he even looked her way. That family was funny to most of us but not to Ronelle.

Mrs. Harris has not been herself since Mr. Harris took sick and passed away. She has been looking like something was missing in her soul for over four years. That is how long it's been since Mr. Harris passed away.

That funeral was a great service with a lot of family support. He was dressed neatly as if he was just sleeping preparing his body for work the next day. I sure did take a liking to Mr. Harris. Everybody looked at my father-in-law as a mean Fred G. Sanford, but he was just protective about his family, especially his 4 girls. He also had 1 boy and his wife.

He had a lot to protect. Mrs. Harris had finally turned over the phone to Nicole as she was saying hello maybe the whole time, I was reminiscing oh shit baby momma thought she lost connection, "Baby, I'm sorry."

I was just thinking about Momma's condition and it brought me back to Roger, that's Nicole's father's name. He took a liking to me, and he told me never to call him by his last name again or he will break my legs. Mr. Harris said to call him dad or Roger; maybe he figured "Mr." made him sound old. He liked the line of work I chose. I guess that's what brought us together. He was a contractor. I'm a contractor too.

Nicole said, "Hello" real loud as I smiled thinking about her parents. "Oh! Hey Baby! I'm sorry." Nicole was agitated now because not only had I blinked out on her mother, but I had done it to her also. Nicole stated with the private eye question, "What are you doing? Where are you? Why you not talking? And so on, so on, yada, yada, yada!"

I began again, "I'm sorry Honey. It's just that I miss your dad. I was listening to Momma, and how sweet of a woman…Roger…" Nicole blurted. "That's Mr. Roger or Daddy to you!" "Well, Honey…He told me to never call him that again or he will break my legs. Besides Mr. made him sound old," I said 'matter-of-factly'.

"Well, I'm his daughter. He's not here," she replied. "And the next time I hear you say Roger again, I'm going to break your legs." I smiled and she kind of had a smile in her tone of voice. As I began, "Woman, you sound just like him but a little softer." I realized I had been sitting in the truck way far too long. The clock now read 6:05p.m.

Troy came out the lane looking impatient flagging me to come on plus I remember the eight o'clock appointment with Charity "crazy ass" woman. I found myself thinking out loud, until my wife asked, "What you say?" As I hesitated, my only response was "HUH?" Nicole said, "What you call me?" "Oh, nothing Honey…" I replied like the TV commercial.

Nicole continued, "Well, I might be crazy but look who my husband is and hung up on that note." Gosh I said, as I looked at the phone call time 22:03…DAMN! I killed the engine and opened the door. Troy was already half-way to the truck.

"Man!" Troy began. "I got to go to work in the morning." "Since when you start working on Sundays," I said. Troy explained, "Man, getting up in my household, Monica would not let off until I'm in the car, dressed for church. That's like getting up for work." As we both laughed, I said, "Tell me about it. Besides speaking of Monica, was that her in the car with you?" Troy looked puzzled. "You saw that?" He asked. I looked at him like 'never mind'.

Troy was always the type to keep at least 12-15 women. Back in college, Troy used to play football for LSU. He made running back. Man, that dude was so popular that other girls at different colleges used to want a piece of him. I mean we would go to the bar after a game and the girls use to be all over him.

One time, we played Oklahoma State University. Troy must have had rushed for 160 yards, 4 touchdowns and over 20+ carries. Man, those country girls would run up to Troy on their way into the locker rooms and just flash their breasts at him. Some might just grab him at his private...What a lucky guy? When Troy went pro, that is when he met Monica.

I guess Monica heard of his reputation with the women and she slowed his ego down when she said she was pregnant, but he still manages to keep about 15-25 women. As we walked to the lane entrance Troy was carrying the case. Troy said, "Hey! I already talked to David, who was the lane manager. "He knows your bringing the case and it's cool?" I asked.

Troy said, "Man, what's my name???" as I held the door for him. We walked into the lane and Troy asked, "Man, what was taking you so long to get out the truck?" "Man," I said, "I was talking to my mother-in-law. She is sick plus Nicole was there." "Oh okay, I can respect that," Troy said. She asked about earlier. "You wanted to talk to me about something?" "Yeah Man," I started, "I met this..." but before I could begin, Troy started, "Man, you know Nicole is going to find out and kill you. Naw, Man. It is nothing like that. I met this woman, right? I didn't actually meet her. I kind of..."

Troy stopped me again, "Man...You slept with her?" "No, Man!" I said. "I was at the gas station and..." Troy started again, "How does she look?" I shouted, "Man, will you shut up and let me tell you?" "Okay! Okay! Okay!"

Troy got quiet and I continued my story, "...so, I was leaving your house..." Troy said "Awh ha!" I went on, "And, I saw this stalled vehicle..." Troy started again with a Wolfman look in his eyes, like a hot and horny dog with his tongue hanging out of his mouth, "You picked her up and brought her home?" "You know what Man? Forget about it!" I snapped. "You are not going to let me finish!"

As I began to walk off, "Let's play man." Troy was like, "Come on man," and were laughing. Okay Tyrone. Man! I was just excited to hear. What happened Man? Come on Man..." As we got by the table, Troy placed the case on the floor behind the chair, Leon was sitting as I shook his and Brent's hands. I said hello to the four ladies that accompanied us. I paused a little, hoping the ladies didn't notice and realized there were four women sitting at the table his boys were at and I began to count on my fingers. Unnoticeable, 3 of them looked at the four of them. Hold up, I thought to myself, where is the fourth man for the extra woman.

As I stood there, not trying to give myself away, because I realized my crazy boys came with some company. As I reached over to Troy, I asked him," should I have brought Nicole, because I'm starting to feel left out?" Troy whispered a very strong, "NOOOOOOOO! Man are you trying to get me killed. Besides why would you bring Nicole if Tara wanted to meet you?" "TARA?" I said out loud mistakenly and looked over my shoulder at the four women and one said, "I'm Tara." I quickly responded with a handshake and "How are you?"

I turned to Troy and said, "I would go and get our shoes. I turned around and let the women know we are going to get our bowling shoes from the truck. "We will be right back. You ladies help yourselves." Troy invited the ladies to the case of Bud Light, and we walked off. Troy picked up on my resistance quickly, "What's the problem?" He asked me. "Troy, you know damn well I would never cheat on my wife." "It's not cheating," Troy said. "We are just hanging out." I started to say, "Man, you know if my wife...Troy...STOP! WAIT..." Troy suddenly interrupted me by saying, "Please tell me that you didn't tell Nicole where we are this evening."

At that point, I had this crazy high school look on my face. "No T!" Troy exploded, "You aren't supposed to tell her where we are. I am extremely disappointed in you," he started. "Hey Troy! You know me better than Brent and Leon. You know Nicole and I have been together for almost 30 years plus you should know how strongly I feel about her. You say hanging out with another woman is not cheating but tell me how you think that would look to Nicole if she came here and saw four women sitting with us and they are all half-way intoxicated off the beer I just purchased at Mal-Mart with her. I'm sorry man but that looks like cheating even if we are just hanging out. You already know you couldn't get Monica to believe that. Man, you know I know Monica."

As we stood in the parking lot, Troy was looking into the sky, he smiled a little bit when I mentioned Monica's name. I continued, "She damn well wouldn't understand that shit. The cops will have to be called to this place just like last week. Remember what happened then? Troy started laughing, "You just had to bring that up. Ok you are right! Now what?" Troy said as we laughed. "What do you want me to do? Tell the two that I brought that we are married and that you are not feeling this Tyrone?"

I said, "Naw Man. They are already here now." As we made our way to the truck, I said, "You might as well let them stay this time, but next time, it's going to be the 'fellas only' man. So, who are the other two women?" "I have no idea," Troy said. "Leon and Brent brought those two." "Okay. That's passable but those other two…that's bad business Man. Troy you're going to get yourself in a whole lot of trouble. One… Monica is going to catch you." Troy laughed at me and said, "Well at least my wife doesn't come and check my whereabouts like Nicole. Hold up, Man! You had to have done something to make her act like that with you," Troy said.

So, you're telling me that in thirty years, you have never kissed another woman. "Nope! And it's twenty-seven years to be exact." Twenty-seven years…Thirty years. It's all the same," Troy said as I grabbed my bowling shoes. I had brought an extra pair for Troy. I closed the back door and locked up the truck. "Really? Twenty-seven years of no kissing or no fooling around on Nicole? Damn!" Troy said. You are a good man. I turned to Troy and told him "I'm a better man than you."

"Oh yeah? Well, if you feel that you are a better man than me, let us just see how much of a better man you are…Let's go bowl against each other tonight. Cool brother?" Troy asked. I repeated to him, "Cool

Brother," but my mind had drifted back to the eight o'clock appointment I looked down at my watch 6.45 pm, 6.46 pm as the time changed. Troy noticed my agitation. "Hey man what's up?" Troy asked. "Why are you looking as though you are in a rush?"

So finally, I was able to tell him about my encounter with Charity. I broke the whole story down to him as we sat at the table. I ended up separating myself from the others and allowing my wedding band to show and made sure I showed absolutely no interest in Tara. I think she got the picture after about 2 to 3 beers and was flirting with another guy at the lane. What a relief I had but then I noticed the time.

It seemed as though it had flown by because it was already 7:40 pm. Twenty minutes until I had to meet up with Charity. Troy was whooping my tail on the score card; I guess I was not in the mood to play after I realized that the time was winding down. I told Troy, "Hey man. I'm going to go ahead and leave out. I promised my mother-n-law I would pay her a visit before I headed out to go home," which was the truth, but Troy knew the story of Charity, so he gave me a look as if to say be careful man.

I told him to call me at 8:15 pm, hoping he would not forget. That way my stay with Charity wouldn't be long. I headed out the lane and got in my truck. Before I even let the engine warm up, I took off 8:05. I was running late. Charity began to call my phone. I knew it was her because she is the only person that calls me private.

As I picked up, she started, "did you forget about our date?" I replied, "No, actually I'm pulling up right now!" The China Wok was never crowded, and that was a good thing. I asked her where she parked so I could park by her. She told me she parked in lane 17. I saw her Toyota Camry there, but I passed it up and as I passed her vehicle, I took down her license plate number and left it on my console and proceeded to park next to her.

I got out of the truck and started walking towards the restaurant. I felt as if I was a rag doll, better yet, a puppet whose strings were being pulled in front of a bunch of little children laughing at me as my legs dangled back and forth, up and down, my arms swinging out of control dancing off the gingerbread man song. As I reached the door, I began to think what if Nicole walked out this door right now. What would you say "Oh Honey, I'm just here to meet Charity, the woman I helped. Or "Oh Honey, I'm not cheating on you. I just stopped by to tell your new client she is making the right decision by choosing to work with you." Or, how about this one, "Nicole, it's not what you think."

As the door opened, my heart dropped into my shoes inside my socks and ran back to the truck. But it was only a couple leaving with a doggie bag. When I walked into the restaurant, everything seemed like it got quiet; like everybody knew me and Nicole were married. I thought I heard someone across the restaurant say, "Hey! Isn't that Tyrone Tucker, Nicole Tucker's husband?" It felt like all eyes fell on me and the music from the record stopped and, in the background, I could see Charity sitting there in a booth instead of a table and she had black horns on her head. Her face was red like the devil and that whole area was on fire. As she opened her mouth and it was as if she was saying "closer Tyrone, just a little bit closer" and as she said that it felt as if I floated right into her arms. I told myself to get a grip; snap back into reality Tyrone, you are going to be okay.

The music started back, the people all started chatting amongst each other and Charity was still sitting in that booth. That gave me a quick chill, as I walked towards her and stood there and began to say you know this wrong right. She just laughed and said," sit down silly," I looked around then looked at my watch 8:20 pm. I began to say to myself this num-nutt forgot all about me; I told him to call me at 8:15 and make like he was my wife and was ready for me to come home now, but he forgot about me or maybe he did it on purpose because I didn't give Tara the time of the day, or maybe just maybe, he would love to see me get into trouble with my wife because him and Monica are on shaky grounds.

Charity said, "Tyrone, the waiter is talking to you." As I quickly snapped out of my trans and began to look up, it was Nicole standing there in a China Wok uniform asking me what I wanted to eat. Twenty-seven years of my life to you and this is how you do me? I stared. Charity smacked the table "Tyrone!" "Huh?" I looked at her as she asked, "Are you going to order?" "No, I'm not hungry." He said, "at least not yet". She told the Asian woman to give him a minute. You can continue my order, as the lady walked off, I said, "What's your problem?" I snapped as if we were a couple, that's when Charity snapped back, "You're my problem."

The other guests glanced over at our table; Charity smiled. Well, just because you're not interested in me doesn't mean you have to embarrass us like this. Now, I can't help," Charity finished, "that I got a thing for you. It's just something you and I gone have to deal with. You are a real man; something I'm looking for." "But I'm married, and I love my wife. I got kids." I argued with this woman. "Ok Tyrone. So, you have been with her 27 years. I feel like I've known you all my life. That little time I rode in your truck with you," I looked at my watch again 8:31 p.m.

That low-down dog, Troy. I can't wait to talk to him. He's probably having sex with both of them dikes he thought to himself. "Why YOU keep looking at your watch?" Charity attacked me with such a harsh tone. "You know what just FUCK IT Tyrone!!" She said while she was getting up.

"I'll just call your wife on my way to the car and tell her, 'Hi Mrs. Tucker. Tell Tyrone thanks for meeting me at the China Wok on Main Street. We had such a good time. This is Charity. The one you met at Mal-Mart. Maybe it will hit her fucking independent ass head on why you really were at Mal-Mart.'"

As I stopped her from getting up, "Hey! Hey! Hey! Charity now, now be cool sit down! Don't be that way." I politely said. She sat back in her seat now listen to me. I never ever gave her a chance against my wife, I'm just a little nervous. My wife knows people, and this is very difficult for me to have another woman sitting where she supposed to be sitting, Charity stated but this was my idea not hers so she's not here where I'm sitting with a little head movement, as she continued you see that's what I'm talking about Tyrone you're the perfect man any woman can ask for. "Tell me," she asked, "how you all made it through."

"Well," I started. "First of all, back in high school, I noticed my wife. She was dating this guy name Ronelle. He was a star quarterback. Headed off to college, him and Nicole. He thought Nicole was going to the same college until she told him she was going to a different college. At our high school graduation prom, they broke it off right there.

Well, he broke it off leaving her at the prom with no ride home. So, I gave her a ride home, as I began to smile, then, from that one ride led into every morning until we went off to college. She went to LSU and, coincidently, I went to LSU also. Neither one of us knew that many people there, so we became friends. Then, one thing led to another and before we knew it, she was pregnant with my first son.

"Wow!" Charity said, "since high school…well college?" "Yeah." I said, "We have been together ever since." She asked, "Do you ever get discouraged?" As I felt her foot raise between my legs as I jumped. She said, "it's okay. I told her, "No! I never had to because my wife satisfies me. She keeps me occupied. Plus, I think it had to do with my parents being together for so long taught me to be a good husband to my wife, a good father to my kids, plus the love at first sight thing."

"Well," Charity asked, "how can you know if someone can treat you better than her if you never gave anyone else a chance to?" As she rolled her foot closer up my crotch, I began to feel a little uneasy while she performed 'semi-foot' masturbation on me. The waiter came back with her food and asked if I was ready to order, I told her that I was ok. Charity said, "Why you're not eating?" I lied and said, "I had a burger before I got here with the fellas."

"Oh really?" She questioned. "Yeah," I answered. I looked at Charity as she stared at me with this look in her eyes. I began to think what a crazy woman she was and how many men had she blackmailed before me; even wondering if she knew who her child's father was. Charity wasn't a bad looking woman, and she had a nice shape but, I was happy with my wife, my kids and grandkid. She seemed like she would be ok if she had a good man. So, I began to think about a few co-workers I could connect her with. She finally moved her foot. "Thank you, Jesus," I sighed. As Charity was eating her Shrimp, Broccoli & Rice, I just watched. It looked really good and I love Chinese food only if it was with my wife. Then, I could really enjoy it.

I looked at my watch when Charity went down for another fork of rice & broccoli. "9:00 pm…Damn," I said to myself as Charity looked up and said "What! Oh! I'm sorry," she began. "Do you want to try it?" As I declined her offer, "No. Thank you. You enjoy yourself though." Charity dug a little rice out and shrimp on the end of her fork. I reached over and grabbed the sample off the fork, to make her feel good, and she picked up a broccoli stem and reached over and said you will need a vegetable with that.

As I pealed it off the fork, she said, "See how easy that was Tyrone? You should get a grip of yourself. It's ok honestly Honey." I, then, said, "You know what? I told my mother-in-law that I would pass by before I go home to check on her. She took sick and we have been taking care of her." Charity said, "you're trying to leave, and you just got here."

I told her, "No, I didn't. I have been here a little over an hour." She looked at her phone and said, "No, I called you. It was 8:06 p.m." She paused and I said "9:10 p.m." I looked over at Charity. I was a man of my word. I came to meet you. You need to be a woman of your word and let me leave.

Charity said, "You were here only for an hour and you didn't eat anything. Your conversation was only about your wife…like I wanted to hear that." "Hey Charity, look you are a nice-looking woman. I'm sure there's a man that would die to be with you," trying to charm my way away from this whole thing. She stopped me, "Well, if I'm such a nice-looking woman, why aren't you all over me to tell me so or show me how nice looking I am?"

"Charity, because I'm married," he stated. "I know that already," she stated. "You are scared I'm going to take your mind off your wife that's why you're scared. I might put it on you that's what it is. No," she continued, "you're scared of young sex." So, I said, "No, that's not none of it. I'm a faithful man to my wife, to my family. I made a vow to God that I will love, cherish & honor…." Charity cut me off, "…Yeah! Yeah! Yeah! All of that holy shit," as she finished her meal. Well, can you at least pay for dinner tonight? Then, I was like, "Sure. I can do that. We both sat there and then tab came and the waiter walked off.

Charity looked at the tab, "Shame! Shame!" As she dropped it on the table, I looked at it. It was only $9.00 and some cent. So, I went into my pocket and realized that I didn't have any money or loose change. Charity said, "What's wrong?" "I didn't bring any cash." She said, use your atm/credit card then. As I went into my wallet and began to fetch my card, I asked her, "You don't have $9.00 Charity? I don't use my card for such petty things like this." She said, "No. You are buying dinner."

Giving her a strange look like I did not recall me saying I was paying for dinner, the waiter came back and asked was everything ok with the meal, Charity said "yes". The Asian woman asked how we were going to take care of the bill. I pulled out my American Express Card the waiter grabbed the bill and Charity told her to take a $10.00 tip. I blurted out, "Like hell she will!" The lady turned around and so did half the guests in the restaurant.

As she walked off, maybe 5 minutes later, she came back with a receipt for me to sign the first thing I thought was my wife is going to get the credit card statement and wonder why I didn't invite her to her favorite Chinese restaurant. Nicole loves China Wok. As I signed the receipt, the waiter walked off and was suddenly stopped by Charity as she grabbed the receipt, pulled her pen out and wrote $10.00 on the tip line of the receipt. At that point, I got really pissed off, but I held my cool and was glad that this was over.

I rushed out of the restaurant. The parking lot still had a few cars there. Charity rushed behind me trying to catch up with me and grabbed me around my neck with both arms as if she wanted me to hug her. She swung in front of me and at that point, I pushed her off of me. "Tyrone!" She said, "if you are mad about the $10.00, I'll pay it back." "It's not the $10.00 I'm mad about." Charity asked, "Well, what is it? I asked, "Were you hungry?"

As I made it to my truck, she beat me to my door and opened it when I unlocked the door. She hopped into the driver's seat. I told her, "Charity, now you are going too far. I'm calling the police." "Oh yeah? You're calling the police? Well, when they come here how about I tell them how you pushed me around out here in this parking lot. A big old man like you," as she grabbed at my private, I pushed her hard. I reconsidered calling the police. She was right.

They are going to take her side and I'm going for a ride. Then, my wife will find out about me and her tonight. I began, "Charity, you need to climb out of my truck. I have a sick mother-n-law to go see after." Charity began, "How about you climb into this," as she began grabbing herself, "and see about making me wet." As she opened her legs revealing she didn't have on any panties, I caught a glimpse but quickly turned my head. She took my hand and ran it across the split of her womanhood. I snatched it back quickly. She was warm and moist which left my hand moist too.

"See…I told you," Charity said, "…hot and ready for you. What you say?" Charity said as she continued constantly throwing herself at me. Just stick it in right here. Just let me feel it. I felt how you were so aroused up in the restaurant. She said, "Tyrone, you know you want me. I can tell you just don't want to go against your vows towards your wife." I thought how my wife is going to be mad at me about lying to her mother once her mother called and asked her where I am.

Charity really hit me with a sucker punch. "Well, I'll see you later," she said as she climbed down from the truck pulling her skirt down after it rolled up her hips revealing her shaved vagina. Then she started again with the threats, "I'm calling Nicole tonight to let her know you out here buying women China Wok and having finger sex with me in her Escalade truck with her picture on the dash." She was walking off and I began thinking that this had to be a crime in some kind of way and, if so, I'm pressing charges in the 3rd degree, 2nd degree & 1st degree. Hell, I want this woman in the "nut house". I knew I was going to hate myself for this, but I called her back. "Charity, wait." She walked back to the truck and I said, "Ok. You win. Tell me when and where you want to go."

Charity said, "There's a hotel. We can go get a room. It's not too far from here and we will be back by 10:00 or 11:00." Man…I'm really going to hate myself for this. I'm starting to hear the judge say, "you stepped out of wedlock and I'm sorry Mr. & Mrs. Tucker that your marriage lasted so long but it took a turn for the worse." My kids are going to hate me; Nicole is going to take me for everything I got. The whole ride to the hotel room was making me feel nauseated. I was doing 25 mph. Taking my time to get there, hoping…in thought…this psycho would change her mind and say, "You know what Tyrone? Turn this damn truck around. I don't want you. I'm deleting your number and I won't call you or your wife ever again."

Yeah right. I looked over at Charity and she looked as if she was feeling me already inside of her. That's when she told me to hang a right. She was ridiculously hot and ready. Then, she said "there it is". I really got nervous because the time is almost there, and Lord knows that I'm not up for this. I began to get dizzy and my head began to hurt.

It felt as if she had a gun on me and was demanding me to have sex with her or she would blow my brains out. I already felt raped. I pulled into the hotel parking lot and stopped at the front office. Charity said the room was already paid for earlier. She planned it the whole time to get me in the room. I can see the desperate look in her eyes; that she wanted me more than ever.

As I pulled up in the back-parking lot, I parked. "This is getting to be very out of control for me," I thought to myself. "You know what," thinking to myself, "I just need to tell my wife about what Charity is doing & take her being mad at me." As long as I didn't sleep with her, I could just tell her everything.

I couldn't get my thoughts together. As I found myself getting out of the truck, Charity was walking towards room #108. As we walked in the room, there was one king-size bed, 1 mahogany dresser, 1 entertainment center with a 52" television inside, 2 nightstands, a room phone & a fancy picture. She had already been in the room. There were candles on just about every dresser top, wooden floors no carpet.

As I stepped inside the room, Charity closed the door and put the chain on. She pushed the lock back and started towards the first candle. As she began to light the candles around the room, she did that as if she had rehearsed her movements.

Once she made her way to the last candle and lit it, she began to slide her left shoulder out of the half lace dress strap. Then, her right shoulder began to slip out of the other side lace strap. As she worked her dress down, beginning to reveal cleavage. Then, her breast popped out from the top of her red lace dress.

I began to get dry mouthed. I have never cheated on my wife. I have never ever gotten this far to seeing another woman's breast. Charity continued pulling her skirt past her waistline revealing her belly button, down her hips, curves revealing her sex as her dress dropped passed her ankles. She was fully naked now. I couldn't believe what this woman was preparing herself to do to me and how am I allowing her to take advantage of me. I'm 209 pounds all muscle & she's only (looking at her) an average of 145-150 pounds.

I went to thinking maybe I love my wife so much to the point I won't allow nothing to get between our marriage, or maybe I knew that as much as my wife question me the minute Charity began telling whatever she could tell Nicole that she was going to believe what Charity was going to come up with to say. As Charity walked towards me, she began at my belt.

Moments later, she pulled me out of my boxer shorts and held me in her hand like she was playing with a slinky. I felt myself getting aroused as she went down, and I could feel the heat from her nostrils and her breath. Charity was ready to perform oral sex on me. She put me inside of her mouth and began to stroke me back & forth. She raised up & began to unbutton my polo shirt letting my jean shorts along with my boxers drop to the floor.

CHAPTER

4

Fifteen minutes to midnight, Sunday morning, leaving out of the room, Charity looking satisfied for her victory of throwing herself at me, walking back to the truck I felt so used to the point that I was feeling sick. As the two of us were getting into the truck my phone started buzzing letting me know I had missed calls & messages.

As I looked at the missed calls; fourteen missed calls from Nicole all over an hour's time; one missed call from Troy. As I raised the phone up to call, Nicole was calling again. I pressed talk. Nicole started as soon as the phone stop ringing on her end. "Where are you Tyrone?" I said, "Leaving Brent's house." Nicole didn't know where Brent lived. She asked, "Why weren't you answering the phone?" "Oh Baby!" Sounding stuck in my words, "I left my phone on the charger in the truck. Honey, what's going on?" "There's nothing going on. I just didn't hear from you anymore since 9 O'clock and that's not like you not to call," she said.

"Tyrone, are you on your way home?" I could hear distrust in her voice. It felt like her voice was saying "You let me down. I will never forgive you Tyrone. Twenty-seven years of dedication and this is what you do to me." I began by telling Nicole I'm sorry and my sorry sounded so sorrowful to her.

Nicole had to ask, "Are you ok?" I had this uneven tone that made her feel like something was wrong; something didn't seem right with her husband; character was stolen from him. As I began by saying, "I'm ok Baby. I'll be home to you in a few minutes." "Ok Tyrone. I'll be waiting on you." Then, those words came, "I love you Tyrone." That was not right for me to allow her to say that because I just went against our love, our vows, our family. All the 27 years we put into this marriage. I remember when we walked out of the church from the alter. When Pastor Moore joined us together, Brother Moore said "honestly" as he spoke to the congregation that "this couple here is a couple from heaven. These two were so unique; it's like they belong together." The church crowed shouted "AMEN!"

But on our way out the church, a voice whispered into my ear "Baby, no matter what, Honey as long as we live, I will always love you!" As I can hear her voice in my heart telling me those same words every day for 27 years, when that phone hung up & her voice left that phone, I was upset with myself. I was in so much of a complete trans, I didn't realize I drove all the way from the hotel to Charity's car.

As Charity was getting out, she said it was nice. "That was nice. I loved every moment of it." I didn't turn to look her way. She said, "I'll be seeing you around." Charity closed the truck door and walked slowly to her car, as if she was reminiscing on that connection between the two of us back at the hotel. I didn't even wait to see her off. I drove through the parking lot, hitting Main Street, on my way home.

At least 20 minutes later, I was pulling up to my house. I didn't even have the energy to pull the truck into the garage. So, I lifted the garage, locked my truck up and walked inside of the garage letting it down. As I walked past the front of the Lexus, the car had a warmth coming from it as if Nicole had not just too long ago pulled up herself. My mind went to thinking silly, what if Nicole followed me???

Thinking about what Troy said at the lane about Nicole and she did she know where I was the whole time trying to see if I was going to be open to her knowing she was still at her mom's. What if Nicole was doing the same thing I was doing but the opposite way around, and just didn't want to tell me someone was blackmailing her. It's not that I would not care because I certainly would care about it. This is my wife. I just encountered the same situation. She would understand.

Maybe she finally let Trenice borrow the car to go to her friend house or something. I stood there in a daze fishing for an understanding on why her car was warm like she had just pulled into the garage from a long road trip from Dallas, Texas to Oklahoma. I walked into the house. The alarm notified me that it was armed and that I had to unarm the system. I only had 60 seconds to do that before it started screaming.

So, I reached up to the dial pad and typed in the code. Then, the system said 'ARMED STAY" or 'EXIT NOW" which lets me know that the house was secured. As the breeze from the A.C. skimmed across my head cooling me down, I turned to my right and looked down the hallway. It seemed like my bedroom door was so far away that it took me forever to get to it. I knew my wife was awake because the bedroom lamp was on plus the T.V. was on too. Nicole was sitting up in the bed when I walked into the room.

I never looked her way, but I could feel her staring at me. Before she could ask me "Where have you been?" I said, "Hi Honey. You've been waiting up for me?" She said, "Yes and I love you." Something about that 'I love you' was sounding so full of sorrow. Again, Nicole said, "Tyrone, I fixed you a steak & potato. You want it?" Thrilled to see her reacting like she would get my food together; I went to run my bathwater thinking this will be the last night I come home late. I let the water run but I felt like slime was all over me, like I was pushed out the back of a garbage truck into a wide-open landfill full of dirty pampers.

The water was running, as I pulled off all my clothes and walked to the dirty clothes bin. I turned around and almost fainted, Charity was sitting in the tub. I began, you are going too far. My wife is going to kill you. She just sat there as if she didn't hear me and her breast were floating in the bubble bath and the smell of my wife's raspberry body wash perfumed the air. When she stood up, her nipples were as hard as rocks. Her curvy body was shining from the suds sliding down her hips.

As she was getting out the tub and walking towards me, I began by saying, "You need to put your clothes on. My wife is in the kitchen. Please don't do this." Charity began to say, "You don't want me?" Then, a voice said again "You don't want to eat?"

When I opened my eyes, it was Nicole standing at the side of the tub. I was in the hot water with no bubble bath and no Charity just

Nicole with my plate in her hand. I began to smile. "Hey!" Nicole said, "You ok? You shouldn't fall asleep in the tub. You can drown like that Honey." I must have dozed off and was dreaming.

My wife was standing in front of me in an all-black gown revealing herself to me. I noticed immediately that she wanted to make love to me. So, I grabbed the plate of food out her hand and sat it on the towel stand. Then, I grabbed my wife around the waist and I just kissed her. I kissed her so gently and lovingly that they seemed as though they could last forever.

I began to take off her gown and there she stood; she was naked and getting into the tub with me. Nicole never questioned me; never pulled back. This is what she wanted of me in the water putting me inside her. She was so warm; warmer than the water we were sitting in.

I grabbed Nicole around her waist as she went up and down slowly, back and forth slowly with her head tilting back in excitement; eyes closed, my eyes closed, enjoying the sensational feeling of my wife; exploring the inner soul of my wife, we lasted for minutes after minutes after minutes. Her arms were wrapped around my neck holding me tightly and moaning my name, "Tyrone, I will never stop loving you. I will always love you, Tyrone."

I just enjoyed the perfume smell she had lingering off the side of her neck. Sitting inside my wife was the best of it all; never coming down she motioned me some more while her chest was sliding up and down my chest, arms still wrapped around my neck holding me tight as ever. Her grip got tighter and tighter signaling that she was about to have an orgasm. She moved faster, more intensely while her grip became lighter and lighter as she let out this moan that she had accomplished her mission. Her goal was complete and that felt so wonderful. Simply AMAZING.

Nicole just set there holding me not wanting to let go. She grabbed the soap and sponge, squeezed the liquid gel onto the sponge and began to wash me. This is why I loved my wife so much. She knew what to do and she knew how to satisfy her husband. I guess this is why we have lasted for 27-years of commitment and if so, she was doing better than me because I had broken the 27-years line when I laid myself inside of Charity.

I could not believe me…What had I done? I had to forget about it. I had to let it go and not carry the darkness around with me. I knew the way I felt about it. I was going to say something one of these days, but not now. Not after what we just experienced. I just couldn't. That would crush Nicole knowing she had put her all into what just happened.

My food was all a front. Nicole wanted me. She wrapped her legs around me to wash my back as I washed hers. We both loved each other so much. Then, I noticed a mark on her neck. It was reddish purple, but I did not know if I had done it, but I did not even care. We continued to wash up, rinse off and let the water out the tub. We both dried off and my wife stepped out of the tub acknowledging how good we were; how it feels like the first time every time.

Nicole let her hair dangle over the mark on her neck, grabbing my towel from around my waist, fondling with me, smiling with this shine inside of her eyes like little fires were sparkling. She kissed me, walked into the room and left me standing in the middle of the bathroom. I wanted to march right into that bedroom and tell her "Baby, I cheated, not necessarily cheated but was forced to have sex with another woman. She blackmailed me. I needed to call the police, but I just couldn't make that move."

I was not brave enough to tell the truth, knowing how that would affect my marriage. My wife will pack up and leave me. Her mom would hate me. Her father may rise from the dead and come do more than break my legs. That man was crazy about his daughters; I cannot say that about his son. The only son he had.

After I finished up in the bathroom, I grabbed the plate of cold food and placed it on the dresser. I sat on my side of the bed while pulling open my underclothes drawer, pulled out a pair of undershorts, a muscle shirt and a pair of socks, I looked at the time. It was passed 2:00 a.m. and Nicole had laid on the bed and fell fast asleep. I looked over and notice she was really sleeping. I got up from my side of the bed and walked toward the dresser. The food looked really good, but I just couldn't make myself eat right then. So, I walked to the kitchen, put my plate back into the refrigerator and headed back to the room.

I crawled into bed, cuddled with my wife and dozed off. Her voice startled me as she stood over me. She was shaking me gently and I opened my eyes. It was Charity. As I did a double take to see where I was, my wife was lying beside me still fast asleep.

Charity crawled into the bed as I whispered, "What are you doing here? What the hell do you think you doing? Charity don't do this!" As she crawled into the bed, still naked and grabbing at me, she put her finger to her lips telling me not to say a word. She climbed on top of me and my wife moved a little without rolling over. I did not hear the house alarm. How did she get past King?

He doesn't miss a water bug crossing the grass. A gecko lizard pisses King off to the point that his bark gets hoarse. I can remember a butterfly landed on top of the fence. King ran toward the fence, as big as this dog is, he jumped on the fence. King stood there looking like 'oh look what I have done!" He knew he had done wrong.

But this woman was in my bed and I did not understand how. I began to say this is a dream. I'm dreaming! I must be dreaming! My wife has not moved one bit and this psycho of a woman is sitting on top of me. Then, my wife rolled over and she still didn't wake up. As Charity continued, I didn't understand how my wife could sleep through this act of unloyalty. Charity began to moan softer, than louder, and louder and louder.

I jumped up. My wife jumped up with me. Charity was gone. I looked around. Then, Nicole asked, "Baby, are you ok?" Sweat was running down my face and a puddle of sweat was settling on my forehead, waiting to roll down to my eyes. As I wiped my face, Nicole asked me again, "Tyrone, are you ok?"

I said out loud, "It was just a dream!" I reached over to hug my wife as she repeated me, "It was just a dream." We laid back down and held each other until she got up to use the restroom. Then, I realized the clock said 5:00 a.m. Sunday morning. I got at least another 5 1/2 hours to grab more sleep. My eyes began to get heavy as I went back to sleep, I could feel my wife as she crawled back into the bed.

The morning sun was blazing through the bedroom window and I could hear my wife getting prepared for church. She began to sing while she was in the shower. She always takes a shower before she goes to church. I never get up as early as her. Nicole had this thing she did every Sunday; she would put it on the gospel station to get the morning word.

My eyes were open, but I was motionless in the same position. She was singing one of her favorite songs by Kirk Franklin. I remained motionless, and my phone rang. It was on vibrate.

Then, it vibrated again. My wife still in the shower. As I rolled over, the clock said 8:45, church did not start until 11:05 a.m. As Nicole was getting prepared, I picked up the phone and pressed talk after scanning the call. It was Troy.

"Hello," I said. "Tyrone man," he began. "I'm sorry I didn't get a chance to call you last night." I stated "Hey man! You let me down man. I was really expecting for you to call me." I was getting ready to tell him about my experience but stopped when Trenice walked to the opening of the door, "Daddy, Momma still in the shower?"

I looked her way and said "Yes. Good morning." She said, "Good morning Daddy. I really need to use her curling iron." I did not hear the shower running anymore. So, it sounded like she was out of the shower. I said to her, "Did you want to check? Knock on the door."

As Trenice walked across the room, Troy was still on the line when I asked him "Hey, are you going to church this morning?" Troy said, "No!" He's going to sit in on this one. He said that he was pretty tired. Plus, it is his turn to cook.

"I figured I would do Sunday dinner and the game is coming on. Green Bay is playing." I asked, "Who they play?" Troy said, "The Saints, of course. You know Green Bay is going to win." I began by saying, "I'm not a fan of Green Bay but I would rather see the Saints win. I love to see the Saints play."

Troy asked, "Are you going to church?" I said, "Yeah, I'm going to go and get the word today. I need it. The devil has been busy this whole weekend trying to overcome me." As Trenice came out of the bathroom following her mom wrapped up in her biggest dry towel, and a towel around her head, I told my wife she looks like someone from Nigeria, Erykah Badu.

Nicole said, "Good morning Honey!" as Trenice walked out of the room & shouted out "Thank you Daddy." I didn't say anything. As my wife closed the room door, Nicole turned and asked, "Who's that?" I looked over at my wife & said "It's Troy." She said, "Good morning Troy," as if he could hear her.

Nicole, Troy and I all went to the same college. Nicole asked me to ask Troy, "How's Monica?" Troy heard her and said, "She's ok." Monica in the background asking him "who is that?" He stated, "It's Nicole & Tyrone."

"Hey Nicole," Monica said loudly. Troy asked, "Did you hear Monica?" I said, "Yes. I told Nicole that Monica said hi." She was trying to relate another message when I said "Hold up Nicole. You have Monica's number. Why don't you call her?"

Nicole gave me a look like she was saying 'oh no he didn't' and flashed her towel open, revealing herself. I said, "Hey Troy, my wife said…" as she convinced me and started laughing. "My wife said is Monica going to church this morning?" Troy gave Monica the phone. "Hey!" Monica started, I said, "Hold on," handing my cell phone to Nicole. As they began to talk, I finally rose up from my bed and walked to the restroom and didn't close the door. The two continued on.

Then, I heard Nicole say, "Hold on," Tyrone your phone is ringing while in the middle of using 'the john'. When she said that, I urinated on the toilet seat. "Oops" and forced the rest up out of me rushing myself to empty my bladder when I heard Nicole say, "Hello."

"Oh shit! It's Charity." I thought "Shit! Shit! Shit!" She called. "Why was she doing this to me? I didn't even know her. I don't want her. I love my wife." I continued as I walked out of the restroom, after wiping the seat.

She said again, "Hello! Hello!" She was sounding frustrated, so I asked, "Who is it?" Nicole said I don't know as she switched back to the other line. "What a relief…" I thought.

"Monica," Nicole said as she continued, "Hey, I'm going to call you from my phone." "Ok." Monica must have asked Troy did he want to finish talking to me. He must have told Monica to tell Nicole to tell me that he would call me back. And they hung up. Nicole turned around with her towel off standing naked on her side of the bed. Nicole smelled so good. I walked up behind her, wrapped my arms around her waist when Nicole asked, "Do you know who that was?" With my arms still wrapped around her, I asked, "Who was that?"

"Oh, that call, Honey?" Nicole began to say, "The call came through 'UNKNOWN' and they didn't say anything." As I unwrapped my arms from around her waist, reaching for my cell that was lying face up on her side of the bed, pressed History, saw the call was 'UNKNOWN'. I said, "Well, Baby. I don't know. Maybe they would call back to speak to me."

Nicole said, "Maybe they didn't hear the right voice they wanted to hear to want to say anything." I turned to ask Nicole what she was getting at and Nicole said, "Well, maybe I wasn't supposed to answer." I began to look puzzled at Nicole's suggestions. My facial expression gave her confirmation that I was getting upset because it seems as if she was accusing me of something.

I put up an argument, "What are you trying to say Nicole? Are you trying to accuse me of something?" I asked. Nicole said, "No! I'm just saying it's strange how someone would call and not say anything, Tyrone. Then it is your phone." As the phone rang again, I answered this time with a loud but attitudinal tone, "Who is this?" But lashing out at Nicole too. "You're trying to accuse me of something if someone calls my phone from an unknown number. Honey, how am I supposed to know who it is? It's an 'UNKNOWN' number," still holding the cell to my face, "Who is this?" And no one said anything.

Nicole began, "That's not what I'm saying. I'm not accusing you of anything!" she shouted, "I'm just saying it's strange, Tyrone but should I be accusing you of anything...maybe I should be," Nicole continued. I was still holding the phone, "Hello!" I shouted. Then, the voice came across, but no words, just a laugh and hung up. "See!" I shouted, "same thing to me!"

"No one because I'm home," Nicole said, as if she did not believe me. I said, "You know what? It is too early in the morning for this and it's almost time for church. We shouldn't be arguing about anything." So, Nicole walked off into our walk-in closet and I went into the bathroom again to wash up.

Nicole began rambling through the hangers in the closet. I felt bad because I knew she was right but didn't want to admit that it was someone I knew; not that I didn't want to tell her. It was what I had to tell her that I didn't want to say. How would I feel knowing we go to church as a family every Sunday together, but I had sex with someone else the night before Sunday school. That would make her so upset. It would also make her change her mind about riding with me to church. She would not forgive me.

I left the bathroom to find my wife putting on her pink blouse and the black skirt was lying across the bed. As my wife was wrestling her pantyhose up her thighs, I began to think about how Nicole was still that sexy high school dream girl. I loved that her figure was still there after having two kids and going to college. She still had her 21-year-old looks, even though she was 41 going on 42 soon.

"Nicole," I said. As she turned to look at me with frustration in her face from not succeeding with the pantyhose, "Look Baby. I'm sorry that we are having a misunderstanding on what we are trying to say to one another. Let's just move on from this. Okay? I'm sure someone dialed a wrong number and was trying to contact someone else Honey." My words always struck with a direct hit to my wife, but deep down inside I knew I did wrong.

I violated against my vows and was trying to help keep her feelings and our attitudes together. I really wish I had the courage to tell her that I made a big mistake, but I didn't. The more I thought I was protecting her, the more I was hurting our marriage. I didn't know how long it was going to stay hidden before Charity decided to step one on this family's toes even harder than she was already doing." I thought to myself, "crazy woman".

My wife did not say anything. After a while, she finally said, "I'm going to take the truck today; you don't have to ride with us." I knew that she was still upset. I walked over to Nicole. She was almost dressed. All she needed was to curl her hair. Once Trenice finished with the curling iron, they she would be done. Nicole never put her pumps on until she got out of the vehicle getting ready to head into the church house, so she wore her pink and white cotton fluffy slippers. I didn't put up a fuss. I just stated, "Ok Honey. The keys are on the key hanger by the door.

As I turned back to let her finish dressing, Trenice knocked on the door. "Momma," as Nicole walked to open the bedroom door, I was standing at the foot at the bed, realizing Trenice had on almost the same thing as her mom. Nicole said, "I'm going to be ready in just a second. I'm gonna bump the ends of my hair and I'll put my makeup on in the truck."

Trenice looked at her momma and turned to me, "Daddy, you're not riding with us?" So, I told her, "No. I'm coming to church a little later plus I still have to get dressed." Nicole was in the bedroom mirror bumping the ends of her hair, I can see the madness in Nicole's body movements, and her actions told me that she did not care about how I felt; she was really upset. So, I let her be and sat down on the bed. Trenice was standing there trying to get a clear picture of what was going on in here. What a way to start your morning! The crazy part is she doesn't want to ride with me to church this time. We always ride to church together. I did not want to argue with her, so I sat on the bed and finished watching her get prepared for church.

I walked to the closet and pulled out a smokey gray 3-piece suit, burgundy handkerchief, burgundy tie, and burgundy socks and laid them across the bed. I had my Fossil gold and burgundy faced watch. Then, I walked back into our walk-in closet to grab a box of Stacy Adams and opened the black leather Z laces hanging from the tongue. The soul of the shoes had a burgundy and black strip going through the inside and was made of cushion that was extremely comfortable to the feet.

My wife was looking at what I was prepared to wear from the mirror; I thought to myself maybe this will change her mind to let me ride with her and Trenice. I walked to the bathroom and picked up the electric shaver and began to sing the song that was on the church radio station my wife left on earlier when she was in the shower.

The clock on the wall in the bathroom read 9:30 a.m. and I was shaving my face when Nicole walked up to me in the bathroom and kissed me on the cheek. "I am going to get Momma and help her get dressed if she isn't already dressed. I have to take the rollers out of her hair and fluff her hair out." I said, "Okay. I'll see you there. I love you Honey." Just by her kissing me gave me comfort to let me feel reassured about our little dispute over a crazy phone call.

As she walked out of the bathroom, she said she loves me too. I continued to shave up my face until it was baby back smooth; a little aftershave and, as I jumped from the tingle, began to get dressed. My wife was still in the house. I can hear her in the kitchen rumbling through the cabinets. As she was headed out, she screamed, "I'll see you at church." "Okay," I yelled back.

Alarm reset, I continued getting dressed and my phone began to vibrate. Reaching for my cell, I pressed talk. "Hello," Charity's voice came across the darkness of the quiet end of the receiver. I walked to the end of the hallway and peeked out the door, the Escalade was gone. "Hello," Charity said, "You're up early." I began by saying, "Yes. I'm always up early for Sunday school." "What church do you go to," she asked. I thought to myself, I will not tell her what church I attend so she cannot come sit next to me on the same aisle as me, my wife and kids. I would not put it past her to do just that.

So, I told her Greater Southeast Baptist. I just told a fat lie. She asked, "Did you enjoy last night?" I wanted to ask her which times, to see if what I experienced last night was a dream or a nightmare, but her being in my bed had to be a dream; my wife didn't move at all.

"Charity, I'm on my way to church," I thought to myself. People used to say Satan sits in church too. And that is all she was...a female Satan. I asked her why she was still calling me. I thought you would stop. Charity says she was thinking about me, how good she felt after getting out of the tub. I could not believe her. She had slept with a married man and was now talking about going to church.

She is such a hypocrite and really crazy. I hung up the phone and finished putting on my Stacy Adams, my Fossil on my wrist, sprayed on some Polo Black cologne, grabbed my Bible, placed my phone in my phone holster, grabbed the blazer to my 3-piece suit and headed out the door.

The time was now 10:20 a.m. I went to open the backyard door to let King in as he was house trained. King was happy to see me, but I would not leave him any food or water. I said to my dog, "Papa's going to church Big Man. Watch over our castle okay?" Patting him on the side of his belly, he is a big dog.

King followed me all the way to the garage door. As I set the alarm to 'ARMED' and headed out the house, raising the garage door and closing the house door leading into the garage, I opened the passenger door. I placed my blazer over the seat, bible on the passenger seat, closed the door, walked around to the driver side, opened the door and got into the car. Nicole sits so close to the steering wheel I thought as I adjusted the seat to my comfort. I sat into the car and started it, thinking to myself "my wife car smelled so good. It reminded me of her so much." As I backed out of the garage and driveway, I let the garage door down and headed to church.

Our service started at 11:00 a.m. It was now 10:45 a.m. and I was driving into the church's parking lot. You have to get to church early to get a parking spot or you will be parking in the far east wing parking lot. That is where I had to park…in the far east wing parking lot. Church service starts at 11 O'clock. It may be the best of all the services.

Church members were walking to and from the house of the Lord. Cars pulling in and out of the parking lot, and a transport bus was passing too. When it passed, a car pulled up and stopped. It was Charity. My heart dropped to my feet again. As she rolled down the window, she said with a smirk on her face, "Greater Southeast huh?" I said to her, "Go away Charity," and walked off.

She laughed and drove off. I kept walking towards the church and made it inside. People were everywhere, and Pastor Harold was on stage giving his opening 11 O'clock service. There were T.V.s on the walls. We had a lot of people today and the ushers were directing people to their seats as I stood there looking for my wife.

When I saw Nicole, she waved me over. I could see an empty spot she had saved for me as I strolled over whispering "excuse me" while walking sideways. Passing people's knees that hung out into the aisle, a lady beat me to the spot and sat right next to my wife. She said, "I'm sorry. Were you about to sit here?" Then, she turned to face me. It was Charity. How did she beat me? She had to go park and all that. So, how did she manage to work her way through the crowd and still beat me here? As she smiled, something about that grin I just did not like?

I didn't like her period, but I couldn't feel like that in church. Then, the bad part is that she comes to sit right here in between, well she moved over to let me sit by my wife but now that put her on the side of me next to my wife, Diva and Trenice. My wife kissed me. "Hey Honey," Nicole stated. Then, I realized her mother was not there. "Honey, where's your mom?" I asked. Nicole stated, "She's still not feeling good." I said, "Ok," as Charity seemed to act as if she was a stranger speaking to my wife & me, "Oh hey Mrs. um," as she paused snapping her fingers directing her attention to my wife. My wife helped her, "Mrs. Tucker." "Yes. Mrs. Tucker. I met you inside of Mal-Mart."

Nicole said, "Oh! Ok.," as she turned towards me and asked my wife, "Is this your...?" Nicole beat her to the punch line "...husband? Yes," reaching out to me her hand pretending like she had never saw me before. I shook her hand very blunt & reached back. I bet she just wet her panties, as I looked up into the sky of church moving over after I prayed to God in thought to send a thunder bolt right through the ceiling to strike her down.

Trenice was giving Charity a funky look like she could see right through her. She began to open her Bible as she looked past me & my wife. She saw Diva. "Hey little precious." Diva leaned over Charity with sky blue barrettes dangling from her head and covered her mouth like she already knew not to talk in church.

Pastor Harold started by having everybody stand. Diva was being assisted by her mom to stand on the bench. This was a huge church as over 6,000 people can fit here. Pastor began to pray for understanding of the word he delivered today, everybody's heads were bowed down. I was looking down with my eyes open, but I could feel Charity watching the side of my head as if fire was burning through the left side of my ear, through my scull and scorching my brain as the prayer finished.

He began by telling the congregation, "Good morning! Good morning everybody! What a pleasure it is to have you here in the House of the Lord. First, let us welcome our newcomers. If you are a newcomer, let's have you stand." All the newcomers stood including Charity. "God bless you," Pastor repeated. "We're glad to have you," and he told the congregation "if you are sitting next to a newcomer welcome them, tell them your name," which Charity already new my name, my everything.

As Charity turned the opposite way from my family and me being acknowledged by the members to her left behind her, in front of her and then she turned to my side of the church. In her face, I could see nothing but evil. Her hand extended out as it turned into an arm of fire in my imagination, scared not wanting to reach out as Nicole reached pass me hitting me with her elbow like 'how rude of you'. Nicole said

"Welcome" still sitting in her seat. As she leaned back to her position, Charity was still standing until the pastor said "Ok. Let's get started."

He acknowledged the newcomers once more & told them to please have a seat & enjoy the wonderful service he has to share. Pastor began by introducing new programs, wishing this day to people whose birthday was today and inviting people to have brunch after the service. He invited the choir to bring their enlightening hymns to the walls and ears of the congregation.

The lights went dim. The music started from the podium and the choir started humming a tune. As the voices began singing, people started to rise and to rejoice holding their hands openly excepting the message from the song. My wife stood up. Diva watched my wife as she sang along with the choir. I stood up. I like to participate with my church.

My wife & I have been coming to this church since Trenice & little Tyrone were babies. We see new faces every week. We have watched the congregation change over so many times; 21 years of faithfulness to this church. Our first pastor passed away during this time.

As the song was wrapping up, Pastor walked on stage. Pastor Harold was only 46 years old. He was the youngest pastor we have had to stand command of this Lord's house. He walked up to the preacher's stand, the podium, and acknowledged how touched the choir was.

As he asked for an applause again for the choir, the cheer sounded of a Saints football game in the Superdome 47-0 Saints' way. He started with the sermon…"Mark Chapter 7 verses 20 thru 23 and he said whatever comes out a man, that defiles a man from within the heart of men proceed evil thoughts, adulteries, formication, adulteries and murders." Then, the pastor stopped and explained how he felt about the passage and began by telling his people about the prostitute who has a black heart to sleep with married men. He even added about male prostitution.

I began to think about Charity; how this scripture reminds me of her and what she is doing. She is murdering my marriage. Then, he continued with how Verse 23 of Chapter 7 from the book of Mark. I said to myself, "It's really strange how God works." My wife was writing, and I had my bible as the pastor preached. I could not believe how Charity was treating me…how she was beginning to be so bold & cocky. How she had me violating my vows in church…

I prayed and prayed to myself. How I would love to rewind the first day when I decided to go to the gas station. I should have waited until the next day. I did not want to be convicted anymore. I wanted to talk to the pastor after service but could not push myself to do it with a lot of people heading up to the pulpit to shake the pastor's hand.

I sat there with my wife while everyone was leaving. Charity sat there pretending she was still writing down today's worship. I knew the minute I get up; she would do the same. Nicole stated, "Honey, wasn't he great? He is always great! His sermons bring forth good messages to his people." As she looked me in my eyes and began to apologize about earlier, Trenice and& Diva walked off from where we were sitting. She saw a few friends she wanted to go speak with them while my wife hugged me.

As I held her, she started saying how much she loved me. I knew, deep in thought, what Charity could be saying in her mind. I bet she had a lot of envious words she was saying in her mind. I grabbed my wife's hand in mine and my bible in the other. She held my jacket and we walked out the church into the lobby as Monica rushed to Nicole. "Hey girl!" Monica said to Nicole as they started to chit chat. Then, Trenice walked up, "Daddy." As I turned her way catching a glimpse of her big belly she said, "Can I talk to you?" "Sure," I said to her as she reached for my hand with Diva on the other side of her momma.

"Daddy, when I was in there, I felt something." I said, "Oh?" She said, "Yes, from that woman. She just did not seem normal. Daddy, you know how you can feel something wrong?" I said, "Yes." Trenice said, "Something about how she looked at Momma; how she shook your hand but how differently she shook Momma's hand." I thought to myself as Trenice kept going, "Did my daughter have a connection with my spirit? Did she feel that animosity I held but she saw how Charity's body language said hello but her other side said something else."

I'm glad my wife didn't catch how she looked like my daughter did because Nicole is no angel; she can get rowdy. Man, I can remember this situation between my wife and this lady next door. Well, the lady lived next door to our house and there was a big tree in the neighbor's yard that used to hang over in our yard. It used to shed leaves on our cars when the garage was broken. That lady had the nerve to get out of line behind our complaint about the tree.

Nicole got mad and made a complaint to code compliance about it. Then, the city had to send someone out to the residence to see what the big fuss was about. The city ordered the lady to trim the tree or they were going to chop it down. Boy was I glad to see them because Nicole was about to get really nasty with that lady.

As Trenice finished by saying "Daddy, that lady was in Mal-Mart yesterday. Momma didn't recognize her, but I did when she spoke to my daughter." Nicole walked up and asked were we ready and said we were going out to eat at our favorite restaurant, China Wok.

I disagreed as soon as I heard China…I quickly added, "Or, we can go to Red Lobster." "Great!" Nicole surprisingly shouted. I asked, "Are we going in both cars or are we going to take the Escalade home?" Nicole stated, "Why the Escalade?" I said, "Because we can use your car." Nicole said, "No, because I don't have any gas in my car." Nicole's face had a smirk on it as she continued, "Come on Honey. Let's bring my car home and use your truck. Please Baby…" We were still standing in the lobby as I said, "Cool!"

Trenice's eyebrow went from joy to hate as Charity walked up. "Hi Mrs. Tucker." Nicole turned around and I took my time turning but not wanting my daughter to pick up on how much I really don't like Charity. Then, she might figure a portion of it. That could turn out bad. Now, all facing Charity. "Hi," shaking my wife's hand. "Yes," Nicole stated. "Excuse me. I don't think you remember me but I'm the woman from Mal-Mart yesterday." "Oh yes!" Nicole said, snapping her fingers with the new beauty parlor.

Charity said, "Yes," and continued for a minute. There I thought she was getting ready to come clean since we were in the church. Instead, she started by saying, "Tomorrow will I need to bring anything?" "Oh," Nicole stated. "Well, I have you set for…" Nicole was looking into the sky searching her thoughts for an appointment date. Charity interrupted by saying, "Well, I thought you set it for tomorrow.

Nicole asked her what her name was again. As she told her, "Charity Hunter…" Nicole continued, "Yes. We are going to need your business information, two forms of ID such as a state license and/or a company name and license." Charity said, "Will you also need my social security card?" "Yes," Nicole stated. Charity said, "I don't have that. I lost it or maybe left it in the City Hall.

Nicole said well that's not a problem at all, but you will need to get it. Then, she asked Charity, "Do you know it off hand?" Charity said, "Of course." As Trenice stared Charity down, looking like she wanted her to look her way so she could ask her what's her problem. My daughter takes after her momma. Nicole said, "7 o'clock pm will be a good time to meet. Put in your application and I'll process it Tuesday morning."

Nicole was talking and I zoned out because I was completely wondering how could this woman be so cold??? How could she just betray my wife and still want to do business??? As the two ladies ended their conversation, they shook hands and Charity went on about her business. She definitely had something up her sleeve. She had me nervous.

For a minute, I felt like she was going to say something to jeopardize my marriage right here in church even as she walked away through the double doors. She is up to something. I can feel it. That was just too much like right; she's getting too cocky. She is actually getting close to my family and that is really making me wonder what she really up to at this time.

This strange lady forced her way into my life. Then, she's playing on my wife's intelligence. After Red Lobster, the family headed over to Nicole's mother's house. When we arrived, the Sunday's newspaper was lying crisply from the sun on the grass. As Nicole stepped out of the car holding leftovers from the restaurant. Trenice was undoing Diva's car seatbelt of the Escalade because we had dropped the Lexus off after our encounter with Charity.

As Trenice helped her daughter out of the truck, she began to stroll behind Nicole. I went around the other side of the truck, stepped on the grass and grabbed the newspaper, and Nicole used her key her mother gave her years ago which was her father's key. We went into the house and it was very well kept up. Thanks to Nicole because she would stop by every morning during the weekday to help her mother with the chores around her house.

Nicole's 3 sisters moved to other states which included the process of finishing college and getting married while starting their own families. Her brother was not as lucky coming up in school. He had a problem keeping his hands to himself and I always knew that one day he would be in jail for that childhood habit. He dropped out of school and began to call himself pimping for a living. When one of his girls wanted out, he brutally beat her into a comma, and she died. Now, he is doing a life sentence without the possibility of parole.

As I closed the door, Nicole yelled, "Momma, we are here! Tyrone is here!" Diva took off to the back room to see her great grandmother as she disappeared around the wall. "Trenice is here Momma." Mrs. Harris never responded. She would always say she would be out but nothing. As I turned on the television to catch some of the sports channel, Nicole walked to the back of the kitchen to check on her.

Trenice was rampaging through the fridge when I heard a scream come from the back room. I dropped the remote and ran to the back bedroom. Nicole was laying on her mother rubbing her head. "Momma," Nicole sobbed "No Momma," as she laid there motionless. I reached for the phone to call for the medics as Nicole just wept. Diva began to weep too because Trenice and Nicole were weeping. Just to see the sight of my 3 lovely queens crying, I began to get emotional myself.

Thinking how my mother-n-law wanted to see me before she passed, it really hurt me deeply to know I was betraying her daughter at that time. In my heart, I was really terribly sorry for my actions. As we waited for the medics, Nicole was taking her mother's death pretty hard. Trenice and Diva finally stopped crying.

I lifted my wife up in my arms and began to say how sorry I was and that it would be ok. It was not easy for me to say but not to have your mother or father, she must feel empty. Her siblings were scattered across the country. Nicole's father's siblings were still alive and her mother's siblings too.

I could now hear the paramedics' sirens coming up the street as the sound of the diesel engines roared right in front of the house. Lights bouncing back and forth in and out of the living area of neighbors' houses. Trenice opened the door as 3 medics rushed right in and one asked "where" and she pointed them to the back room.

As two-way traffic over the radios of the EMTs' filled the house, I heard more sirens coming down the street and the city cops blocked the street. The neighbors began to come out of their houses to see what all the flashing lights were about. Everybody knew Mrs. Harris. They all came across the street to check on her. The neighbors stood on the sidewalk on both sides as Mrs. Harris' best friend came running up. EMTS were escorting Mrs. Harris out at the same time.

Mrs. Linfield was coming through, "Claire!" Mrs. Linfield scream out in her elderly voice. "What's going on as she walked on side of the roll away bed, barely keeping up with the technicians. Cries filled the air as Nicole came rushing out the door to her momma as if her mother was calling out for her help.

As she collapsed at the end of the driveway, I rushed to her aid. The neighbors were already there to assist her. Nicole took this extremely hard. I reached in and grabbed her from the arms of the people who helped her to her feet. I had tears in my eyes as Trenice stood in the doorway crying as the medics rolled the bed back into the truck.

One guy turned around and asked if Nicole wanted to come. Nicole rushed out of my arms, to the truck and got in. I hurried to my truck and I told Trenice to stay here; watch over the house. As the medics rushed up the street, Mrs. Harris was not moving. She was dead. The medics pronounced her dead in their truck on the way to the hospital. They tried everything they could to revive her for the last fifteen minutes.

The medics were turning the corner and my flasher was on. The medics ran the red lights and so did I. This routine continued all the way to the hospital. Pulling up in the emergency unit driveway, the medics handed over a clipboard for the receptionist to write out some information. As we rushed to the back in an ER room, doctors and nurses joined the side of the roll along bed straight through the double-doors that read I C U.

We prayed that they would revive my mother-in-law. Please Lord. Nicole rested her head into my chest. I cannot allow my wife to be hurt anymore. I will carry this dark secret for the rest of my life; I don't have to say anything. As we sat in the lobby, the clock on the wall read

10:15 p.m. when the doctors came into the lobby where my wife and I slept. I was holding Nicole in my arms when the receptionist came in and brought us a sheet to cover up. The nurses were genuinely nice. The doctors came in and said, "Hello Mr. and Mrs. Tucker." Nicole jumped up from my arms and rushed to the two doctors who were standing before them in the lobby.

"Mr. and Mrs. Tucker? Yes!" Nicole said. "Can you please come this way?" Both of us walked side-by-side with the doctors. As we went into the double doors, we were both hoping and praying that the news they were about to give was that she was saved and was doing fine on a breathing machine. That they were going to keep an eye on her under observation to watch her condition, but the doctors' words snapped me out of my daydreaming session.

"I'm sorry," they said in unison. As Nicole broke down in tears, her knees gave out from under her and she collapsed in my arms. The doctors continued, "Mrs. Harris passed at 10:41 p.m. That is when I said the technicians told us she was dead when we found her. The doctor said, "We were able to revive her, but her illness was so severe that every procedure we were trained and educated on did not work over a 30-minute period.

The last time the administration was provided it did not last over a period of seconds. I am sorry," he said. Nicole stated, "Is there any kind of way you guys can let her live on some kind of machine until my other siblings can get in town to tell her goodbye?" "I'm sorry Mrs. Tucker. She just did not have the strength in her to even hold the serum that revived her lungs so she could accept the oxygen that it put out to keep her revitalized. I am so sorry Mr. and Mrs. Tucker. My name is Dr. Kovisky and this is Dr. Armstrong. You can visit your mother's body if you would like as she is still in ICU and we will start the paperwork and death certificate completion.

Nicole came around a little to hold herself up, still the tears were falling. Her eyes were bloodshot red, and they were baggy that if she pressed or blinked wrong, a bucket of water would spill from them. I was hurting also but I had to be strong for my wife.

As my cell phone rang, "Hello," I answered. It was Charity. Then, I hung up. As we made a left following down to the north wing, 3 big red letters were stenciled across two double doors that read I. C. U. The hallway seemed as if it had gotten longer as if we were walking through a tunnel. The closer we got to it, the longer it felt.

Nicole's cell phone rang, "Hello." It must have been one of her family members because the minute she answered Nicole broke down again trying to say, "Momma's dead." She could not get it out, so she passed me the phone.

I put it to my ear. It was one of her sisters. I could not recognize the voice due to the emotional breakdown beside me and inside my ear, that is when I said "hello" again. "Who is this?" "Tyrone," the voice erupted it was Katrina! She lived in Chicago. "Is it true?" She asked. "Is my momma dead?" I began to swell up as the tears came from my eyes. "Yes, Katrina. She passed this morning." I heard a thud as if she dropped the phone or maybe she fainted.

"Hello! Hello! Hello!" I repeated. Another call was coming through as I tried getting Katrina's attention. It was no use. I could hear her whaling in the background. I clicked over and a man was on the other line. I knew this voice. It was Uncle Matt. Matt was a truck driver and was in town. He heard the news and he sounded sad and a little broken up from his findings that his older sister had just died.

He wanted to know if we were still at the hospital with her. I told him "yes sir" and he wanted to speak to Nicole. Since he could hear her crying I the background, he changed his mind. He said he will be by the house because he did not want to come to the hospital.

I told Uncle Matt that my daughter and grand baby were at the house. He said okay and I told him we would call once we were about to leave the hospital.

Nicole walked into the room. There were nurses with Momma as she laid on the table under a white sheet. The nurse had tears in her eyes to see the presence of Nicole's condition, full of emotions. The nurse excused herself from the room as I entered, Nicole was pulling at her mother's hand as if she was telling her to get up; let's go Momma but my mother-in-law was motionless.

Nicole's tears flowed like water as she struggled to get the first words out, "Ma-Ma Momma. I'm sorr- sor-I'm sorry Momma," as if it was her fault. She sounded as if she was blaming herself that her momma passed.

I tried everything Momma. I tried everything. You didn't warn me. You just left me like this…" as her words became so emotional, "I cou-could have gotten you to the hospital Mo-Mom-Momma." Sounding like a little baby all over, Nicole's words fluttered in and out, so heart touching that I could not help but to break down myself. I could not hold it. I sat in the chair, put my head in my lap and exploded into fury. My tears poured so much that my shirt was drenched.

Nicole came to my comfort and I just whined and whined until she touched my head and said, "Baby, it's okay. It's okay, Tyrone." I began, "If only I- I- I would've come like, like I promised her. Honey, she wanted to tell me something," pausing and wiping the snot off my nose like a two-year-old boy.

"I should have," as Nicole touched my chin, raised my face up and said she understood. "She called me baby." Amazed from the control Nicole had of herself, she came around when the double doors opened. Dr. Kovinsty, Kivisky whatever his name was came in and stood there for a moment respecting our grief as Nicole turned with tears in her eyes. The doctor said, "Mr. and Mrs. Tucker, I'm sorry. I know how you must feel. I lost my parents, and I was devastated. So, yes, I know how you feel right now. But look at the bright side, your mother was a good lady and I have treated both her and her husband.

They both always talked with love and compassion very sweet, so I know this isn't the time to say this, but she lived her life, and she would want you all to move on with your lives but keep her in your hearts. Nicole was pleased to hear her mother's doctor say what he had just told her, and she hugged him. As they released their grasp, the Dr. had tears in his eyes. He walked out of the room while Nicole and Tyrone viewed their mother one last time and headed out to start on the funeral arrangements and to make phone calls to family members on both sides.

The ride back to Momma's house was quiet. As they pulled into the driveway, Uncle Matt was there along with a few more relatives. That's when I looked over at Nicole and asked, "Are you going to be okay Sweetie?" Nicole said, "Yes. I'm going to be okay." She took a deep breath and looked through the windshield at some of the neighbors who were still hanging on the front lawn to offer support to Nicole and her family.

CHAPTER

5

Monday morning seem to take a long time to come for Tyrone as he laid in the bed looking at the celling. Nicole was asleep when I rolled over to face the nightstand. The clock read 4:17a.m. My wife tossed and turned all night until she finally went to sleep. I knew how she felt to lose a mother. Her father passed over 4 years ago, her brother was in the penitentiary for the rest of his life and her sisters were scattered across the states.

I could not go back to sleep, so I got up and went into the kitchen to start up a pot of coffee. I have to go to work in a few more hours, so a nice pot of hot coffee will suit me fine. I went into the dry food pantry to get the best coffee in the world; my grandfather introduced it to my father: Folgers Roasted Blend Coffee.

I love the aroma that it sends out. After about 7 minutes, it began to fill the house. My wife loves Folgers Coffee too. I think King loves Folgers too because he was standing on the window seal staring into the kitchen. He is a big dog. King's face was so big, it looks as if he was a baby bear on four legs.

I turned the alarm off and opened the door. King rushed around the corner of the house; jumping up on his back legs so I could rub him. His front legs were on my chest. I began to talk dog talk. He was so happy. King was like my second son; he loved me. I think if I was to let him go, he would find his way back home. He is the only dog I know that cannot resist being away from Nicole or me. Trenice does not like him; she never did. But my son loves him.

As I walk over to the dry food pantry, he already knew what I was thinking because he beat me to the door. Seems like he was telling me his bowl was empty outside. There was a huge scooper inside the bag that measured up to 7 cups. As he put his face into the bag, I told him, "No King! Down bad dog…" As he backed out of the closet, I scooped a glob of dog food onto the scooper; whatever I dropped, he would eat it off the floor. It happened every time.

So, I went from the kitchen to the backyard. It was still dark in the sky, very early in the morning. As I poured the dog food into the bowl, I grabbed his water bucket and rinsed it out because it was full of grass and dirt. I filled it with water from the water hose on the side of the house and walked it back to King's eating and drinking area.

As King gobbled through the food and drinking water once he had a mouth full of food, I went back into the house, closed the door, set the house alarm back and opened the bread box. There was wheat bread; almost a loaf left. I opened it and grabbed at least 4 slices. Then, dropped the slices into the toaster. When first Nicole bought this device and brought it home, she paid $40 for this thing. I was so upset because out of all the toasters she could've chosen, she chose the most expensive one. I hated this toaster for almost 3 weeks until I noticed how golden brown it made our bread, now I love it.

As I smiled, I pulled out the blueberry cream cheese. My wife loves cream cheese. She was the one who introduced me to it over some years ago. The toaster beeped and golden-brown toast popped up and the toaster automatically turned off.

I put two saucers around the center of the kitchen counter, which we use it as a breakfast bar. It sits in the center of the kitchen with 8 stools around it. My wife also has this thing for gadgets; she said less mess. She also had a processor that could turn anything into juice. I didn't need it but Trenice left it on the bar when she used it to make Diva's orange juice. So, I put it back where it belongs as I boiled 4 eggs.

I went back into the bedroom. My wife was up early and singing in the shower. I walked in as she was wrapping up. "Good morning Honey," I stated. Nicole smiled. Her naked body was so sexy; she was truly the apple of my eye. As I approached her, she reached out for the warm hug that I was about to bless her with. She just melted into my arms with her head on my chest. Then, she jumped back like she smelled something horrible on me.

Nicole said, "Have you been around King?" I laughed, "I'm sorry Honey." Then she stated, "Folgers Baby?" She smiled. "Yes Mam," I said. She walked into the room, grabbed her gown from the foot of the bed and slipped into it. She sprung right towards the kitchen, holding my hand. "Wow! It smells so good in here Honey. What you got going Tyrone?" Nicole asked. "I did a little something for us Baby."

When we reached the kitchen, there was toast on the breakfast bar, blueberry cream cheese, coffee in the pot ready to be served and boiled eggs ready too. She smiled and hugged me, "Baby, I love you so much. You sure do know how to put a smile on my face." I blushed. I always cook for my wife when she was not in the mood. One time, I made some shrimp etouffee.

I was taught by my stepfather. My biological father was not around. My stepfather had been in my life since I was maybe 3 years old or a little younger and he was a certified chef for the Holiday Inn Hotel for over 20+ years. I learned a lot from that man far as how to be a man. This guy got up every day and went to work. I watched him do this same routine for most of my life until I went to college.

Nicole pulled out a bar stool and sliced her toast in half grabbing the cream cheese and a butter knife. I took the pot of coffee and placed it on top of a hot pad that sat on the bar counter. As we sat and discussed the arrangements for Momma's funeral, Nicole asked if I was going to work this morning. "I don't know," I answered. She asked me why and I told her that I figured she would need my help. "If not Honey, I can, definitely go to work."

Nicole said she appreciated me, but she did not need my help. If she did need me, she would give me a call. I smiled as I bit into my toast smothered in cream cheese. She took her finger and wiped the mess from my mouth. I was glad to see my wife being so strong about this; that's what I loved the most about her...how strong she is. But I still could not fix my mind on being straightforward with her about my encounter with Charity; and now was not the time to do so.

As I grabbed my coffee mug and strolled over to the flat screen T.V. that hung on the wall of our kitchen, I powered on the device. The 5 O'clock news was coming on at that time. I reached back and grabbed a bar stool. As I sat there, my wife was writing on a message pad that sat by the cordless phone on the wall. The commercial quickly bored me, so I headed towards the bedroom after stuffing a boiled egg inside my mouth and chasing it with hot coffee.

I went into the closet, lost in thought, then headed back towards the kitchen where I disarmed the house alarm system. I entered the garage where my work clothes normally hang after Nicole had washed them. She would normally hang my work clothes here because of the chemicals that the fibers held. As I slipped into my leather jean suit, my steel toed boots were there too, along with my welding helmet, gloves, and all my supplies I needed.

As I was gathering up everything, I walked to the visor of my truck and pressed open the garage door. I began putting my work equipment inside the back door and closed it down. Then, I walked back into the house. My wife was still sitting at the bar writing, but on the phone, maybe with one of her relatives. I kissed her and told her to call me if she needed me. It was going on 5:30a.m. and my shift started at 6 O'clock. I worked 12 hours shifts from 6 am until 6 O'clock pm, sometimes longer.

I went back into the bedroom to grab my cell phone and my watch that laid on the nightstand. I grabbed all my belongings and headed to the garage to go to work. Before leaving, I called out to Nicole, "I'm gone Sweetie." She acknowledged, "Okay! Be careful and have a nice day." I closed the garage door and hopped into my truck and backed out, letting down the door of the garage, and pulled out my phone and placed it on the mobile the charger.

As it automatically powered on, halfway into town, my phone rang. "Hello." "Hey Tyrone. What's going on?" It was Rudolph. "Oh, good morning Rudolph. How is everything?" He began by telling me what his weekend was like and how excited he felt about the new project they had started. Then, he asked me how mine was.

I started by telling my story, then after telling him our family's biggest lost, he didn't want me at work for the rest of the week. He seemed broken after I told him about my mother-in-law. I remembered when my wife's mom had a cookout for all the site supervisors & foreman. When Rudolph met my mother-in-law, he fell in love with her but was respectful towards Mr. Harris, my father-in-law at the time. So, not only that he gave me a week off, but I was also promised to still get paid for that week.

After hanging up with my boss, I turned my truck around and headed back home. My phone rang again. "Hello," I answered. "Good morning." As I recognized the voice, my blood began to boil. I felt overheated from her presence on the phone. "Hey, Charity. I'm not in the mood right now to be talking to you." "What's wrong Tyrone? Did you enjoy yourself at Red Lobster yesterday?" I couldn't believe it.

Well, I could believe it...she was a stalker. I just remained silent, trying to figure out how to get rid of this woman before she destroyed my marriage. I cannot allow that to happen. So, it was time for me to kick into gear with this woman. I needed to be playing alone with her game, playing that same game with her until I could break her.

My wife's family will be here this week along with mine so I can't allow her to play me like a puppet on a string. From Saturday, something had to give as I responded, "Hey. What are you doing up so early this morning?" Her voice kind of changed after she realized that I was speaking civilized to her.

Charity talked with excitement, "Well, I was up getting ready to take Rene to school." Just playing along with her, I asked, making as if I was trying to get to know her, "What school does Rene attend...high school or middle school?" Charity said, "She's still in middle school. She goes to Millennium Middle School. She is in the eighth grade. She's a great student...very smart." Not like her momma, I thought to myself. She asked to meet up, but I told her I was on my way to work and I do not get off until after 6 O'clock. I started heading to Millennium Middle School. I could hear that she had not left her home yet.

So, when I arrived and spotted her, I followed her home so I can know where she lives and start doing her like she was doing me. It was time to fight fire with fire. I could hear her and her daughter talking, so that let me know they were still at home.

After ending our call, all I needed to do was wait at the school and spot the white Toyota Camry with the license plate number 809-FR6.

Just sit and watch from Lowes across the street. The time now read 6:50 a.m. Parents and school buses were pulling up and dropping off children for school.

Then, right before my eyes, the Toyota Camry pulled up into the school parking lot. I needed to get a closer look. So, I drove across the street. The license plate matched. Then, I saw her; hopefully, she did not see me as Rene stepped out to the curb to chat with a few school friends. When Charity pulled off, I waited for a few cars to pass then followed her. I was hoping she would call me so I could figure out if she was going home, are not. She was just cruising. I thought for a second she saw me tailing her, but she didn't.

I was caught by the red light and Charity was getting further & further away. I began to curse as the light turned green. I gave my truck the gas, all the way to the floorboard, but once I saw I was approaching her vehicle, I slowly let off the accelerator passing through another stoplight as it turned yellow. Charity was still a little way up, but I kept a good distance from her so that I would not be noticed tailing her. She put on her right blinker and it stayed on letting me know she was getting ready to make a right turn on Wind Brook.

This neighborhood was somewhat the ghetto. As she made a right, at least 1 minute and 5 seconds behind her, I made the same right as she kept straight into a curve around the street, I followed her. She turned into a driveway. There was another car in the driveway. I began to wonder if this was her husband's car. Maybe she was lying the whole time. As she got out the car and walked toward the front door. A man opened the door and seemed like he was leaving.

As I drove past her residence, he kissed her, and he walked to his blue SUV. I glanced back at the license plate. It read C71-10A. I took the first right. Her address read 1217 Wind Brook Lane, so I turned around and started to head back to watch the man leave. The truck was headed back to the main highway. Once I noticed the truck had left, my phone rang, and I scanned my caller I.D. It was a private number.

"Hello," I answered. It was Charity and she asked, "You busy?" "Yes. Kind of…" I answered. She said, "I'm going to meet up with your wife today." I frowned then asked her, "Where are you?" Charity replied but lied, "at the grocery store." I knew she had been lying to me the whole time. I was looking at her car from where I was sitting.

I asked her to meet me at the China Wok parking lot for lunch. Charity agreed but wanted to know how come I was being so nice all of a sudden. Then, she asked what time it was in a sarcastic way. I thought to myself that she should know the time since she was home. After about 5 minutes into the conversation, she began saying how she wished she could see me now.

In my mind, she was playing games and I knew it now. I know that she has a man and hopefully I can get the tables turned without her trying to get my wife involved. The time now read 8:06 am in the morning and Charity's car had not moved since she arrived back home or since we hung up. Then, something occurred to me...Maybe she has been watching me at the corner of her street where I waited for her next move. So, I decided to move along since I had her address now, both vehicle license plate numbers and now I needed a plan.

I have already set a date up with this psycho bitch, but I did not put anything together. I need to think of a master plan. How can I stop her rampage without causing a scene or a problem? I just want this to be over.

As I approached the stop light, I thought about calling Troy because he knew people. He had cops for friends, and I had tried talking to Troy, but his mind was on being with other women all the time but me and Troy had been best friends since college. I thought about it over & over before I realized I was calling him. When Troy answered, he sounded as if he was still asleep. "Hey Troy! Wake up!" I shouted! I need your help on something.

Troy wanted to know what the problem was. So, I started to say, "Remember the psycho stalker I was telling you about?" Troy said, "Yes." Then, I asked where Monica was, and he paused. I guess she was still asleep. Troy did not have to work. He was living off his NFL money and Monica did not work either as he said to me right here.

I continued with asking him about a few of his cop buddies and what could I do to stop this woman from tearing my marriage apart? Troy wanted to meet at my house a little later after he could find out something about what I asked him. I told Troy, "Man, I can sure use your help. I need to get this woman off the streets." As he yawned into the phone, Tyrone said, "I will call you back in a minute," which was his way to end the phone call.

I headed towards my house so I could check on my wife. Twenty minutes into driving home my driveway was occupied by two more vehicles. I suspected it was my wife's siblings who were in town, so, I parked on the curb but from the remote on my sun visor, I opened the garage door.

I killed the engine, exited the vehicle, locked it and headed into the house. The commotion let me know it was family members. The garage main switch was at the house door. I hit the switch and as the door was letting down and I walked into the house. Her sister was sitting at the breakfast bar, there was a guy sitting in my den and I approached him. He was looking down when I walked up.

I scared him because he jumped a little when I acknowledged him. I introduced myself; his name was Mark. I let Mark know who I was, and I welcomed him into my home. Then, I walked into the kitchen where my wife was still sitting in the same place where I left her this morning. She was startled by my entrance.

"Hey Sweetie," I spoke as she smiled and said, "You scared me. Tyrone what are you doing here?" I began to tell her what my boss did, Katrina spoke, "Hey Tyrone!" Then, she asked, "You meet my friend? He's in there." "Yes, I met him," I responded. Nicole stated, "I have contacted just about half of everybody," which means I need to get a hold of my family. Nicole thanked me for doing that much to help.

The doorbell rang. My wife got up and headed towards the front door. When Nicole opened the door, I could hear her talking with someone in the front room. As she walked back to the back of the house, I didn't see who was with her. When she came back, she had the welcomed company with her and had followed my wife into the kitchen. It was Charity. My wife introduced Charity to her sister. Then, turned and introduced me to her which I already knew her very, very well. The psycho stalking woman nodded her head my way smiling.

"Well," Nicole stated, "I was quite sure I set your appointment for 7 p.m. but since you're here, we might as well get things started. But do you have a minute," my wife asked Charity. I am still doing things for the funeral. Charity said, "Take your time." "Did you bring the information I need to get your application started?" Nicole asked.

Nicole was a real professional about how she ran her business. In this part of her life, I was incredibly surprised how she was handling things, how she was still willing to work at a time like this. I guess she knew she had to be strong but when her father passed, she took his death really hard.

I knew it was going to hit her sooner or later after all the arrangements had been completed for her mom's funeral. So, I knew I was going to have to prepare myself for her emotional deadline. Charity continued to search through her purse for all the documents that Nicole had requested. Charity brought out 3 forms of IDs and handed it over to Nicole.

Katrina looked at my facial expressions which gave her a bad taste in her mouth. That is when Katrina asked Charity what part of town, she lived in. When Charity folded her arms and said east side of the city of Dallas, I knew she was lying. Katrina attacked her again, "What kind of business are you trying to open?" This time, Charity got a little out of hand and asked her, "Why all the questions?"

Katrina looked as if she was seeing straight through Charity and replied, "I'm sorry Sugar if I offended you and besides it's none of my business what you do. That's your business." With that, Charity looked over towards me after rolling her eyes at Katrina, and asked, "How do you do Mr. Tucker?" Nicole turned around noticing the smirk on Charity's face and that didn't sit right with her. Charity had this look on her face as if she were thinking, "You lied to me; you said you were at work plus you wanted to meet up."

My blood started boiling, sweat started rolling from the hair line of my head and I noticed the look my wife had on her face after catching a simple smirk on Charity looking over at me. When she spoke, that is when I stated, "Fine Mrs…" as I could not remember her last name.

Charity helped me out by saying Mrs. Hunter. "Yes! Mrs. Hunter," I repeated hoping my wife did not recognize my nervousness. As I proceeded to head out the kitchen, my wife said, "Tyrone, since you are about to leave, why don't you take Mark with you do the man thing?" I turned and agreed to Nicole's idea as I was leaving out the kitchen. Charity said, "Nice meeting you Tyrone," as I kind of paused but kept going.

When I made it to the den area, I noticed Mark was gone. So, I went back into the kitchen and told Katrina that Mark must have left. He's not out there. Then, I asked, "Does Mark live in Dallas?" asking Katrina. She immediately responded, "Yes!" But Charity was actually eyeballing me. I noticed her stare but turned like I didn't recognize it.

I headed towards our bedroom to use the bathroom, looked into the mirror and then strolled to the closet to change my clothes. I grabbed a Polo shirt and a pair of Polo shorts since I already had my Polo tennis shoes on. After changing into fresh clothes once I removed my work clothes and smelling like Issey Miyake cologne with my Polo gold watch, I headed out the door.

Nicole walked up to me and kissed me. I looked at her. Charity was staring behind her as if she hated my wife for kissing me which I didn't understand, but, in due time, my wife was going to hear the news. So, out the door I was going when Nicole grabbed my hand and pulled me back to her. She whispered in my ear, "Don't make me cut her."

I knew it was coming the way she looked at me in the kitchen and my wife caught her, but I never responded. So, I headed out the door. I was letting up the garage when my phone rang. It was Troy calling. I pressed talk on my cell phone and answered, "Yo Tyrone!" Troy spoke. "I got a partner of mine on the phone and he's a cop." As I acknowledged him, a strong voice came across the receiver; I stood in the middle of the garage.

The cop said, "I hear you are having women problems." Then, Troy began to laugh. After realizing he laughed at his friend, he apologized once he noticed no one else was laughing. The cop continued, "The name is…" Then Nicole opened the door. The cop said, "Hello. Hello," repeatedly. As Nicole stood in the doorway, "Tyrone!" she shouted.

"Troy," I said while ignoring my wife, "I will call you back. Let me talk to Nicole," as I turned to walk back to Nicole. She was so beautiful. "Yes honey." "I thought you already left," she stated. "I need you to come and see what's wrong with this computer."

I walked back into the house and into my wife's office, there were certificates everywhere her college degrees hung across the wall, state license certificates, my wife had her name plate on her desk.

I remember when I bought her the ink pen holder, I smiled, Charity was sitting in one of the black cushioned office chairs that my wife had picked out from the Office Outlet. Those matched her black burgundy looking mahogany desk which matched the scenery of the office.

I tapped on the keyboard I can feel Charity watching me real hard through those evil eyes of hers, nothing happened after tapping the keyboard. So, I pressed the power button on the computer monitor. Nicole said, "I did all that Honey."

I moved her chair back. The front square of the desk was made cut out. As I bent down to check the plug, Charity's legs were half opened until she realized I was on my hand and knees. She opened her legs wilder revealing she didn't have on any panties. Then, I said while under the desk, "Honey, the plug isn't plugged into the outlet." So, I connected it and heard the computer kick in. Then, the fan started.

As I was coming from under the desk, Nicole was standing directly over me, with her pretty golden tan legs; I played around her legs making her giggled a little. "Stop Tyrone. I got a client here. Maybe later." Then, Charity exhaled a little to catch my wife's attention.

"Okay," I said later right looking over her shoulder then I hugged Nicole, Charity had a look on her face that didn't sit well with me. All I could think of is her spilling the beans and my wife ripping all her hair out of her head and then letting King eat on her for his lunch. I got a bad vibe from Charity.

Nicole raised from my grasp and laid a nice kiss on me. Charity said, "Did you all get the computer up and running okay?" Nicole turned and said, "Yes. It's actually downloading now. Would you like a cup of coffee?" "No," Charity quickly answered. Something in her voice made Nicole's eyebrow turn up.

"Okay," Nicole exhaled. "Well, thank you Honey." "Thank you, Tyrone," Charity followed. Not liking how she called my name, Nicole asked her, "Are you okay Mrs. Hunter, because you seem a little over the edge? Do we need to reschedule?"

Charity sat there. I was nervous. Here it comes. She's about to tell it. "The way I see it," Charity said, "well, I will just put in the application and you can get to processing it. Once we do that, you can give me a call with the quote."

Nicole did not understand why she was changing her mind but said, "Okay, Mrs. Hunter." As I was leaving, Nicole waved bye to me. I walked out of the office through the hallway, out to the garage when Katrina emerged from the kitchen, "See you later Tyrone."

I closed the garage door behind me. Then, out the garage to where my truck was parked along the curve, the spot was empty where Mark had parked. I unlocked my truck, opened the door, hopped inside, pressed the button and the engine fired up. The AC began to blow cold air out the vents as I sat there.

When Charity came storming out of the house, Nicole came behind her along with Katrina. Trenice was at Nicole's mother's house with Diva. The two ladies were having a disagreement about something. I could not make out what they were saying when Nicole walked towards my truck. "Tyrone!" She shouted, as I rolled the window down, she had the nerve to tell me my price was too high and started cursing at me.

"What's her problem?" Katrina started towards Charity's vehicle. I jumped out of the truck, "Wait Katrina! You can't sister. If you fight her, she will sue Nicole. So, you really don't want to do that."

"You need to check yourself," Charity said, "and your prices because if you expect for me to pay those prices, it's not going to happen." Katrina was Nicole's youngest sister and she wanted to lash out on anybody that was causing any hardship than what they were already experiencing. Charity pulled off and Nicole looked as if Charity done more than just turned her down.

She looked at me and walked off. I didn't know what that look was basically about, but I really needed to know. I needed to know but not from Nicole. The explanation needed to come from Charity. I kind of felt the tension in the air.

I turned off my truck, locked it up and went back into the house. Nicole was walking back and forth in the den. She was upset when I walked in. So, I walked over to her and hugged her as she broke down with her face in my chest. I knew it was more than just the misunderstanding between her and Charity but more about her mother's death was taking its effect on her now.

I began telling her that "It's okay and that it might seem like everything is tumbling down on you, but you are doing great. Your mom is okay, and she is in a better place; she has been reunited with her husband plus she is looking down on us all. Baby, it's okay." Nicole was really hurting, and she said I was only trying to help.

They don't even look at it like I was helping. "Baby, you are doing great." I continued trying to bring comfort to her plus I brought up her offer about our bedroom date. She started snickering and calming down as we just stood in the den area holding each other. Katrina joined us. When my cell phone began to ring, I just held them both.

I felt like Mr. Harris. I had to play that father figure to his daughters beside the rest of the siblings were not there yet. My cell phone was constantly ringing. I knew it was Troy from the ring tone. When Nicole noticed I wasn't going to answer, she backed up from my grasp, and she said, "You can answer Baby."

So, I reached down after Katrina backed off. "Hello. What's up Troy?" As I listened to what he was saying, I told him about my wife's mother's passing. He got quiet as if he knew what my household was going through. Troy said he would call me back. I hung up and Nicole said, "I'm going to finish putting together the service."

Katrina said, "I'm sure going to miss my momma." My wife walked off into the kitchen. Katrina fell back on the sofa. As I walked off, I called out to my wife, "I will see you in a minute Sweetie. I'm going to meet up with Troy. Then ride and look for a few funeral chapel locations." My wife shouted back, "Okay. Be careful."

My phone rang again as I was leaving. Charity's voice came across the receiver and, in a flash, I asked "What are you trying to do?" Before I could continue, she began by saying I'm a lying ass man and that she thought I was at work. Plus, she thought they were supposed to meet for lunch. "I wanted to tell your wife how we fucked…" she went on.

Before she could go any further, I stopped her and asked her where she was headed? Charity did not respond. Then, I stated I wanted to meet for lunch at Applebee's or Denny's. Once I got her to agree to meet me at Applebee's, I hung up. Then, I called Troy and told him to have his cop friend stake the place out on Hwy 80 for a better chance to not put my marriage in jeopardy. So, when it's all said and done, my wife would believe me when I tell her I was getting blackmailed by this woman.

CHAPTER

6

Back at home Nicole and Katrina was leaving when a blue SUV pulled up & Nicole got out of her car after telling Katrina to wait a second, walking up to the tinted blue SUV the window rolled down as he smiled hey sunshine Nicole smiled back Royale was an ex-client until he went back in business for himself Nicole taught him everything, she knew about the insurance business. Then, he started up his own.

Nicole asked, "What brings you on this side of town?" "Oh," he said, "I was just passing and saw your car and decided to show my face. I enjoyed dinner Saturday night even though you didn't eat anything off your plate." Nicole stated, "Well, I was just leaving to set up my mother's funeral services." As Royale sat back in his seat, amazed at what Nicole just told him, "Well yes!"

Nicole, noticing his reaction to what she just told him, said "Yes, my mom passed yesterday." Royale, still sitting back in his seat with his head resting on the headrest of the driver's seat, staring at the windshield in a daze. As he turned back to Nicole, he said, "I'm very sorry to hear that Sweetie. Is there anything I can do to help?" Nicole smiled, "Nah. I think between me and Tyrone, we have covered everything."

Royale's voice kind of did a little switch when she mentioned Tyrone. Nicole said, "Well, thank you Royale for stopping by to check on me. I got my sister in the car waiting on me, and we have a lot to do. I will give you a call later." Royale made a hand phone signal telling her to call him as he began to slowly pull off. C71-1OA his plate read.

Nicole returned back to accompany her sister who awaited her return. She asked Nicole did she hear from Tameka or Shawna and she wanted to know if Roger was going to attend Momma's funeral. Nicole stated, "Shawna called before you came Katrina, plus Shawna supposed to get in contact with Tameka and I don't think that prison will let Roger come to the funeral." Katrina exploded what "Um hmm?" Nicole murmured, "He has life and the warden told me this morning he don't think the governor will allow it." I asked him if he could at least try, and he said he was going to call me back.

Katrina said under her breath, "That's messed up." Nicole shrugged her shoulders as Katrina asked, "Who was that in the blue truck?" Nicole smiled and said, "An ex-customer." Katrina poked her lips out and said, "Tyrone is going to kill you Girl."

When Nicole was pulling out of the garage, her phone rang. "Hello Mrs. Tucker." "Yes!" Nicole answered. He began to speak, "My name is Dr. Kovisky. We spoke on yesterday at the hospital." Nicole said she remembered, so the doctor continued to speak. When he invited Nicole to the hospital to speak with her, she began trying to figure out why Dr. Kovisky wanted her to come by the hospital.

He continued by saying further that he would like to speak with her back at the hospital and she hung up after saying thank you. Nicole told Katrina that she was going to the hospital. "That was Dr. Kovisky. He was the Dr. that pronounced Momma dead and now he wants me to come to the hospital."

Katrina asked "Why?" Nicole hunched her shoulders while saying, "I don't know." So, she headed to the hospital. For the next 20 minutes, the car had a long silence between the two women. When Nicole turned left and arrived at the hospital, she found a parking spot. As the two women exited the car, they walked to the entrance. They noticed a pretty young white lady who sat behind the desk, the receptionist. When she looked up and asked politely, "Can I help you?" Nicole said, "I'm here to visit with Dr. Kovisky."

The receptionist picked up the receiver and dialed Dr. Kovisky's extension and said, "Dr. Kovisky, someone is here in the lobby to see you." After the receptionist hung up the receiver, she said, "Dr. Kovisky will be here in a minute." Then, she asked if we would like some coffee? Katrina said no and so did Nicole. When Dr. Kovisky arrived, maybe 5 minutes later, he said, "Hi Mrs. Tucker." As Nicole turned to face Dr. Kovisky, he reached out his hand and said, "Right this way please."

The three of them walked down a marble white glass clean floor. They turned right into his office from the hallway. He pulled out two chairs and requested the two have a seat as he strolled around his desk and sat in a burgundy leather chair. His office had plants that looked like elephant ears plus a mahogany desk with doctor's degrees, hospital certificates, trophies for surgical awards, a picture of 5 men holding an exceptionally large fish they had caught and family pictures.

Dr. Kovisky was searching for a file. Once he located it, he opened it up and began telling Nicole about her mother's autopsy. "What our hospital coroners found was pretty unusual. After dissecting your mother, we found a chemical that was in the blood line that was not a biochemistry agent. It was a chemical unbalanced compound serum that separated the blood and was injected by a syringe. We ran tests on the serum, and it appeared to be morphine. Both women began looking puzzled as they were trying to understand what the doctor was telling them.

When he began giving them the information about the injection, the tears came flowing. As the doctor stopped to assist both of the emotional women, he continued explaining how sorry he was for their loss. Again, Nicole stuttered her words as she said, "So someone murdered our momma, but why and who would want to hurt our momma?" Katrina began to cry louder as she held her face in her lap. The doctor said, "We don't know if someone injected your mother with the morphine or if she did it herself."

Nicole shouted out loud, "My momma didn't do any drugs!" As the doctor continued to try and calm Nicole and Katrina down, he knew this was going to be difficult for the family to handle and an exceedingly difficult thing to explain especially since Mr. Tucker was not accompanying the women. Nicole began in a baby sigh, "Once again, who would do something like this to our momma? I had just left her. Trenice, Diva and I went to church; she said she wasn't feeling good. She was going to finish up on her rest. And my momma didn't allow no one inside her home, not even Mrs. Linfield, her best neighbor. She had been a friend of the family since I was a little girl.

As the emotions began to quiet down, Katina just sat in her seat, tears flowing down her pretty fat checks. Nicole was trying to be strong, but her eyes began watering up again while muffling out her words. "Dr. Kovisky, is there any kind of way we can find out if it is true that our mom was murdered?" "Well," Dr. Kovisky stated, "we had a medical examiner perform more studies after finding this drug in your mother. I'm your mother's personal doctor and after her last checkup, we never found anything in her blood stream. Her heart rate was not normal, and it looked as if she suffered a heart attack due to the insufficient blood that did not supply her heart after the administering of the drug."

Nicole did not want to hear anymore. She began to get up as if she were about to leave. Dr. Kovisky leapt from his seat, "Wait Mrs. Tucker. You have every right to be upset and yes, I want to help you find who did this to your mother, but I don't want you both leaving under pressure. Let me help."

Nicole stopped at the door along with Katrina and she stated, "Doctor, there is nothing you can do here. We have already lost." Dr. Kovisky said, "You ladies deserve justice for your loss; besides, I knew you mother personally. I know she was not capable of drugging herself; she hated needles. I literally needed my nurse's assistance to help administer her medication. You have been there, Mrs. Tucker. You could witness how your mother reacted when we had to give her medication. You see, I feel as though she was attacked. Being your mother's doctor, I want to go beyond my license to catch the perpetrator that did this to your mother." Nicole wanted to cry but had to be strong for Katrina as she could not hold her emotions as she cried and cried on her big sister's breasts.

As Nicole held her, Nicole told Dr. Kovisky that she's going to get a detective on it immediately. Dr. Kovisky, for almost the fourth time hurting to see the two ladies in their emotional stages. The two women left the office not in the same mood as when they came into it.

When the two reached the parking lot, Nicole phoned her husband. Before getting into the car, she stood outside the car waiting for Tyrone to pick up the phone.

Back at Applebee's, Tyrone was accompanied by Charity when his phone began to ring. He had a special ringtone for Nicole as well as Troy. So, he knew it was his wife calling when he picked up. Nicole began by saying she got a phone call from the doctor. "He wanted me to come by the hospital to explain his findings of the cause of death of my momma," she continued.

Tyrone didn't understand so she cut through the chase when she exploded that the doctor was saying momma was murdered. That's when her tone of voice caught Charity's attention. Charity studied Tyrone's facial expression.

Tyrone said, "Calm down Honey. I'm on my way home right now," but Nicole was on her way to the police station to file charges for murder so a detective could start investigating her mother's murder.

"That's a great idea Baby," Tyrone stated. "Well, I'll meet you at the police station." Then, as Nicole asked, "Where are you?" Tyrone froze but answered immediately, "I'm over at Applebee's having a drink." That's when Nicole began to argue about her mom's death and how she's doing everything to get it solved and she started at her planning a funeral while I'm having drinks and hung up.

I felt very guilty, but I had to stop Charity from ruining our marriage and I had to think of something really quickly. As I dropped twenty dollars on the counter for the waiter and began to get up to leave, Charity asked, "Where are you going now? We just got here."

"My wife is having problems and she needs me." Then, Charity started saying, "You are full of shit. I knew I should have not come in the first place." She got so upset she stormed out before I knew it. She had made it to the parking lot, gotten in her car and peeled off.

I didn't know what to expect now, but what I did know was that she had a husband, and I had a tape on her to start blackmailing her back.

When Officer Swiss pulled up, I was standing by my truck. He handed me a disk. I handed him $100 bill and he asked, "What's her problem?" I said, "My wife told me that the doctor called and said the autopsy report came back for her mother today. She didn't die of natural causes. She was murdered. Since I was getting ready to leave, she got mad and stormed out of the bar.

I hope there's enough on this disk to blackmail her back so she can leave my family and me alone forever. Officer Swiss asked did Nicole make it up to the precent yet because he had a friend who worked in homicide. I told him I didn't know but I was going to call and find out. She was going to file charges.

Swiss got on the phone and dialed a friend of his while I got on my phone and called Nicole. Her phone just rang without her answering. Then, she finally picked up. I said, "Honey, a police friend of mine is sitting here in front of me calling a friend of his at homicide." Swiss said, "We'll have her jump on the investigation immediately."

Then, my wife told me to come home and I said I was on my way. I told her, "There will be someone from homicide contacting you as soon as possible. Her name is Detective Kimberly Abrams. I'm on my way home." As we hung up, my wife did not sound as if she was happy to hear that I was moving fast on getting a detective on the case as quickly as I did.

I let officer Swiss know to contact me later once he received an answer from Detective Abrams. I walked off from the unmarked unit towards my truck and hopped into it. Without hesitation, I started the engine and pulled out. I felt this strong sense of sadness for my wife. Her whole life, she felt like everything had fallen apart, so she needed me at home at this time in her life.

I looked at the clock. The time was 2:27 p.m. and the day was getting hotter. As I drove down the highway, getting ready to exit when traffic came to a halt. I couldn't believe I was not focused on the traffic ahead. I could have detoured from this highway if I had been only paying attention. I had too much on my mind. Something is going on, up ahead someone wrecked their vehicle. My rearview mirror showed red and blue lights gleaming about four cars back as the police car was riding the shoulder of the highway.

When I got to my exit, it was 3:12 p.m. Almost one hour stuck in traffic. Nicole was calling again. I passed the collision then I answered, "Hello Honey." "Tyrone, where are you?" Nicole asked in a calm but tiresome voice. "I'm coming. I was stuck in traffic thanks to the idiots that blocked all 3 lanes on the highway after colliding with each other. It was a 4-car crash; two cars were rolled over on their side, another hit the guardrail with another slammed into the back of that one.

After explaining what happen on the highway, I let her know where I was, and I would be there in about 5 minutes. Then, we both hung up. As I was turning onto my street, I could see my house from the main street. An unmarked car was parked in the front of my house. As I arrived, I got out after turning off the engine, walked into my house using the front door after realizing that it was half cracked open. I entered my house.

There was a slim lady looks to be in her early thirties white lady holding and writing on a clipboard. When I went in, my wife jumped up and ran right into my arms. Holding me, Katrina must have gone home because her car was gone. I guess all the bad news drove her away, the young white lady jumped up from the leather sofa of my den she reached out to introduce herself, Hi Mr. Tucker. I'm Detective Abrams. I will be working on your wife's mother's case. I can tell that she was respectful and smart at what she does. I don't think my wife ever had to deal with a detective ever. She began to ask questions.

"Mr. Tucker is there anything you can share that will help this investigation?" "Well, Detective Abrams, I spoke with Officer Swiss." She smiled, "Okay, you met my husband." I must have smiled a little because Detective Abrams said, "Yes." I guess she said that because Swiss was black. "So, that's who referred me to your case?" "Yes," I said. "He told me about a good detective he knew. I'm a good catch," as my wife blushed a little still in my arms.

"Well," Detective Abrams trying to get back on track, "I don't have nothing to share. The last time I spoke to my mother-in-law was Saturday. I was supposed to visit her, and I didn't before she passed away." I began to feel tears flowing down my face. I feel so guilty about my dark secret, and why I had not lived up to my word.

Detective Abrams said she was going to try this case at the best of her abilities. The way she looked at me is like she could see straight through me. It was like she knew everything that I did wrong on Saturday after 8:05 p.m. She wrapped up her meeting as she walked back to her briefcase, grabbed the handle, and placed the strap over her shoulder. She asked Nicole if there were someone over at her mom's house and she said, "My daughter and grandbaby were there along with my mother's brother."

The detective asked for all their names. Nicole started, "My daughter's name is Trenice Tucker and my uncle's name is Matthew Harris, my dad's brother. They should still be there, well maybe not my uncle. He is a trucker so he might be gone but my daughter is there. She's pregnant; she's not going anywhere." Detective Abrams smiled and asked, "What is she having? Do you know?" Nicole said she is only 3 months along.

Detective Abrams walked towards the door, turned with a card in her hand and said give me a call if anything else comes up, and, left saying she would be in contact. Nicole and I walked Detective Abrams to her unit. She turned and thanked us, then, entered her unit after putting her bag on the passenger seat. She blew her horn and left. Nicole looked at me with her lonely eyes as if I was the only thing left in her life besides her kids and siblings. I looked down at my wife standing almost 2 feet taller than her. I told her I loved her, and everything was going to be alright after placing my arm around her shoulder as she placed her arms around my waist.

We strolled back towards the door. King was standing by the fence wagging his nub. He had no clue of what was going on, just full of excitement. I turned and asked my wife to come with me. Let's take King for a walk. My wife was not in the mood to take a walk. She said she just wanted to relax, take 3 Tylenols and take a hot bubble bath with a vanilla mocha. That sounded good.

"Well, I would walk with you," Nicole continued, "but you're not going for a walk either,' and she grabbed me around my belt loop and said, "you have to stay with me. You're going to wash my back. You're going to recharge me." As I smiled, Nicole was inviting me to her. As we walked into the house, Nicole's phone that she had left on the table was ringing. She rushed to it, picked it up and said, "Hello." It was Trenice. She was crying. Nicole said to her to "Calm down, Baby. It is going to be okay. I'll be over there to come and get you Honey. Did Uncle Matt make it back there?" She said, "No."

Nicole said, "When he arrives to give me a call." Trenice must not have understood that I wanted her to stay there and watch over the house. "There is a detective on her way there. She's coming and her name is Detective Abrams. She is coming to look around okay?" So, Trenice must have agreed to stay a little while longer. I told Nicole to tell my daughter I love her & my grandbaby. Trenice heard me. That's when Nicole said, "They love you too."

Nicole rushed off the phone. We walked into the room; Nicole went into the restroom to run her some hot bath water. The raspberry bubble bath aroma filled the air as I pulled out the CD case to put on some Frankie Beverly. The lyrics filled the air meeting that raspberry fragrance. The sound and smell put together was love in the air. My wife really needed me right now. I could tell by the tone in her voice.

For the last 24 hours, she was a pipeful of pressure at 110* degrees over ready to explode, and at that time, I was her only depressurized tool she could use to release that pressure off her. I went into the kitchen after finding myself singing 'After the Morning After', going into the refrigerator finding some of the best Moscato red wine. The wine was never opened, just sitting in the back of the refrigerator.

King was standing inside the window seal and he scratched to get my attention. That dog loved me so much. I think if he were standing in the window seal at the time of an intruder being in the house and fighting me that hunk of a dog would jump through that window to help me or Nicole. Because he was such a big baby towards us. He knew how to get our attention. I remember one-time Trenice was outside fusing with her baby's father in front of the house, King was in the yard. He jumped the fence to go and attack the little guy but good thing I was watching from the window.

I saw when King jumped that fence, so I rushed out the house and shouted, "Down King! Down right now!" King stopped and looked back at me. Then, he looked at Trenice and Diva's father as if he were saying that man right there was hollering at Trenice and he was going to bite him.

The little guy made it to his car before King could get to him. I smiled and I had no clue of what was going on. All I knew was that I saw King jump a 5 1/2-foot fence at his size then. That let me know that I needed to raise the fence level higher than where it currently was sitting. Our fence is now 7 ft tall, so he cannot jump that or dig under it.

Nicole began to call me. I grabbed the two empty glasses and looked back at King as I said, "Big fellow, I will see you in the morning." I rushed to the back of the house back to my wife who was in the tub. She was soaking in some raspberry water, a towel around her head, Frankie Beverly soothing the air space.

When she looked up, she saw the bottle of Moscato and two glasses; she reached for the glasses. As she smiled, I began to say, "Hold up Honey. I'm going to set the mood and set the glasses on the countertop where all her make-up was plus the wine bottle. She said, "Honey, I love you." As I began to undress, I was down to my socks and boxers when I reached into the pantry; there were potpourri pieces in a bag. I grabbed the bag and poured some on the floor, into the water and on the seal of the deep country tub that was custom built.

She smiled and said, "What are you trying to do?" Answering herself back that southern ladies' smooth soft voice of a woman said, "You are trying to make me melt all over you Tyrone. You're trying to make me give you another baby, Tyrone!?!"

I kind of frowned but knew that wasn't going to happen. As she smiled, her beautifully lined up pretty white teeth were ivory white; she seduced me from a distance with licking her lips. I felt a nudge inside of my boxers as they came down to my feet; stepping out of them, removing my socks and towards the "battle" tub I went.

Nicole stood up reveling her perfect body for a woman in her mid-forties girl your ass I couldn't finish what I wanted to say that's when her lips met mine. Her tongue collided with my tongue, her wet warm body next to mine as if the two bodies had minds of their own. Love was transpiring between the two hearts; felt like our hearts beat the same rhythm. Then, she rubbed my body, and I rubbed her body. She was holding me in her hand, masturbating me, her eyes were closed as if she had traveled to another time zone. I rubbed her soft cheeks, grabbed a handful, her kisses lasted a lifetime; I enjoyed them.

She began to speak, "Tyrone, I love you Baby. I needed this," she said as if she was whining for me. She pulled at me masturbating back and forward as I took my tongue and ran it down her neck like she was a giant caramel ice cream cone. Her neck smelled of raspberry fragrance. I was slowly working my way down her neck, to her shoulder, nibbling at her. She smiled with part of my tongue in between her tits.

Her nipples were stiff as I was putting my lips around them letting my tongue work every sensitive part of her breast, caressing them in my strong hands, working them as they slipped through my grasp. My knees began to bend and fold working my way down to her belly button, kissing her until I reached her womanhood. Her hands rested on my head motion after motion. She followed me and she followed me round and round she swirled; my tongue was massaging her deep spot. She rubbed her hands around my head like a fortune teller, this is the woman I loved to give passionate romance to I thought to myself. This is what real love is…when you have a wife. My wife was the other half of me.

I began to climb into the water, and she wanted to do the same thing to me, but I refused to allow her to do that. This is your moment. This is what she longed for…a peace of mind.

I sat down in the water as she sat down on me finding me to insert me inside of her. She moaned the first time it touched her warm deepest spot. She rocked back and forth very slowly; rocking backwards and forwards as her nipples looked like bullets ready to go off. A few times I sucked at them while she rolled side to side. We must have danced all evening in the tub.

Almost an hour passed, and the water was cooling down. I stepped out the tub, opened the cool bottle of wine and poured some into the glasses while watching the bubbles sizzle from the bottom of the glass to the top of the wine line.

Nicole sat in the sudsy water full of bubbles. She relaxed as I grabbed the barbecue grill lighter and began lighting the candles that sat around the restroom. I turned off the light, sat back in the tub handing Nicole a glass as I sat behind her in the tub.

When she laid in my chest and began to sing along with the music floating in from the bedroom, I could still feel my wife on me. She was lying on me in deep thought and I just held her as she said nothing. I knew she was thinking about her momma. I knew she knew that I was hurting but she needed me to be strong for her.

CHAPTER

7

Trenice was making Diva a grill cheese sandwich when the doorbell rang. It scared her a little as she jumped, she ran to the door to look out the peephole and saw a young white lady and two men. Trenice softly said, "Who's there?"

Detective Abrams introduced herself and her two partners who accompanied her. Trenice was already informed about the detective so she opened the door and there stood three strangers. "Hi," Detective Abrams began. "Are you Trenice Tucker?" Trenice nodded yes as Diva came standing on the side of her mother leg. Detective Abrams looked down to greet Diva. She hid behind her mother in fear of the three strangers. A smile came across Trenice's face for her young daughter's action.

Detective Abrams said, "This is Louis, and this is Rodriguez. They are both crime scene techs. I spoke with your mother and father." Trenice stopped her, "Yes! They called to tell me you were going to pay me a visit." Detective Abrams said, "Great! Well, I guess we're on the same page." As Trenice stepped aside, Detective Abrams complimented the scenery of the well-kept home of the former Mr. & Mrs. Harris. Pictures of family were hanging along the walls, sitting on the tables, inside of bookshelves, and the china cabinet was filled with chinaware.

The house still lingered of the coconut fragrance that Mrs. Harris used to polish her cherry wood cabinets, Chester dresser drawers and parts of the linen cotton stuffed wooded 3-piece sofa set. Trenice told the investigator she would be in the kitchen if they needed her for anything. Diva continued to watch the three while following her momma back into the kitchen. The crime scene tech was in out of the house with different equipment. As they set up, the two technicians began putting on masks and latex gloves.

They began in the room where Mrs. Harris was found. As Louis walked in the room noticing the window opened. He began to dust the window seal after noticing leaves and dirt that was freshly sitting on top of the carpet. With the camera around his neck, he started taking pictures of the dirty carpet. He took a picture of the quarter inch cracked open window after pulling the special tape from all the parts where he dusted for prints.

Rodriguez was taking pictures of the bed and stepped on a little orange cap that belongs to a syringe. He took a picture of the object, then he picked it up with his latex gloves and placed it inside of a plastic bag. He raised up when something caught his attention; it was a handkerchief. A little glass bottle unwrapped from the cloth. Rodriguez called for Abram to come see what he discovered, a little bottle that had a strange odor that lingered off the handkerchief.

Detective Abrams came in with her badge around her neck and a 9mm Barretta on her shoulder holster, "What you find guys?" Rodriguez began by holding up a plastic and pointing at the handkerchief with the bottle. Rodriguez said he found it under the bed when I pulled it out. This little bottle fell out of the handkerchief. Detective Abrams knelt down, picked up the handkerchief with the tip of her finger and smelled it.

As she jumped back, a pretty strong odor was released. "What do you think it is?" Abrams asked. "Well, from what I can see, this cap belongs to a syringe and this bottle and handkerchief must have been used as a smothering solution. It looks more like a knockout gas to keep her from screaming. This syringe needs to be tested for drugs. Detective!" Louis called as she was acknowledging Rodriguez of what that hanky smelled like…fingernail polish…as she walked over to him.

This window was a quarter inch open as if the perpetrator came through here. Abrams said, "Maybe she left it cracked." "Well, that's not likely," Louis argued, "because the dirt from the carpet shows entrance from the window seal unless she climbed in the window to open it." Detective Abrams looked down at the dirt. It almost revealed a shoe print, but she really could not tell, but there was a print visible. Abrams reached into her pocket and grabbed a pair of latex gloves. She placed them on her hands and opened the window to look at the other side to see the ground; just what she suspected.

On the other side of the window, Mr. and Mrs. Harris was mud but not much. Detective Abrams told them, "Continue on Rodriguez." As the detective slipped out the room door, down the hall, back into the living area and out the door to the side of the house. When she stopped and looked down for footprints, she followed the folded grass until the path turned into slight mud. One footprint was revealed. As Abrams knocked on the window, Louis opened it. She said, "Tape measure and camera?" She measured the size of the footprint. It read "7 ½; such a small foot," she spoke out to Louis.

Then, she took a picture of the print along with the measuring tape still open reading the print with a close up shot so the picture can read better the size of the print. She did that with length and width of the print. Detective Abrams said as she stood up, "I'm really starting to think of this being a female shoeprint from the actual size. Well!" She sighed handing back over the camera and the tape measure.

Then she said, "How about dusting this side of the glass to get prints from this side too? Louis was walking along side the bed and saw more dirt tracks which led from the window to the front of the bed to the closet. He took pictures of that also and went outside to the side of the house, where he took fingerprints of the outside glass.

It was a very noticeable set of prints after administering the white dust that most lab techs call magic powder. The handprint revealed was very small. It was obvious that it belonged to a woman, but if not, it was the print of a very small man. Detective Abrams began thinking "…If it was a woman, what made her commit such a crime against harmless Mrs. Harris?"

Nighttime began to break through, and the crime scene techs were wrapping up their investigation. After packing everything up, Detective

Abrams was sitting in the living area when Louis and Rodriguez walked up with the equipment in hand and peeling off their latex gloves.

Rodriguez sighed, "That's it. We ran everything. Now, all we need to do is get back to the lab and run more tests to find out what we got." Detective Abrams got up, after handing Diva her WordPad game back, and said, "Well, Trenice it was nice chatting with you. We will see each other again soon. Trenice led the team to the door. As she closed the door behind them, she felt a little comfortable now that they were gone.

Detective Abrams and her team were packing up their equipment when Mrs. Linfield, the neighbor, walked up to the crime lab van. She scared the heck out of Abrams, Mrs. Linfield was a little old lady who looked to be in her 70's.

How can I help you Mam? Mrs. Linfield apologized for scaring the detective, she started talking her old voice had a creepy tone to it. She said, "I'm Mrs. Linfield, a friend of Mrs. Harris and I have been knowing the family since God knows how long." She pointed with her little fingers over to her home and said, "I live there, and I saw a lady walk over to..." but before she could finish, Detective Abrams stopped her and pulled out her notepad and pen. Then told her to finish.

Mrs. Linfield said, "I saw a lady get out her car. She had on a black dress with a brown paper bag in her hand. I took it to be strange because I know all the family. I don't think I ever saw this person before. She went to the front door, then her living area window and finally to the side of the house. I realized the strange action the lady was doing..."

Detective Abrams cut Mrs. Linfield's words short, "What strange actions are you talking about?" Mrs. Linfield said how she was looking through Mrs. Harris's house windows. Abrams began to write that down as Mrs. Linfield continued, "Then, she ran around to the back of the house. That's when I called the police. The cops that came did not make it in time. I didn't want to get in the way of the lady; she could've had a weapon. I didn't know." Detective Abrams just listened.

"So, did the forensic techs???" Then she stated, "The lady was on the side of the house for at least 30 minutes, so I got a chance to write down her license plate number." Mrs. Linfield handed over a piece of paper with the vehicle plates on it. **"C71-10A,"** as she continued, "it was a grey or was it? I can't remember the color, but I know it was a utility truck looking thing." The detective then asked Mrs. Linfield for her name and contact number.

As Mrs. Linfield requested for the detective's pen explaining the only way, she would be able to remember her number was if she wrote it down. "I'm getting old," she said. Detective Abrams smiled as she handed her the pen. Mrs. Linfield looked up towards the sky like she was searching for something as she began to write. Then, she handed the pen and pad back as Detective Abrams in return reached her a card telling her she would be in contact.

The techs walked to their van. Then Abrams walked to her cruiser as the two government vehicles pulled out and vanished down the street. It was late. Back at the police station, Detective Abrams was getting ready to wrap up her paperwork when Louis came in her office with a yellow folder in hand. "I got the results back from the medical records department," Louis said walking up to the desk.

"Wow! That was quick. What about the prints?" Louis handed over the folder and Abrams opened them. "Nicole Tucker, Claire Harris, Diva Scott," the detective sighed. "This is the victim's..." she whispered. "This is the victim's daughter and Diva Scott is a family member. I'm guessing that we need to question the two. Is it anything else we can come up with? What about the window prints?" Louis said, "There's nothing."

"Damn it! Well, that is the only lead we have. Is the Diva Scott character??? Abrams began checking her notepad, looking for the name, Diva Scott. No Diva Scott. Then, she clicked on her mouse in the criminal search database and typed in Diva Scott. Nothing popped up from the search.

A white car pulled up at the Tucker's residence. After a figured exited the car with a red gas can and a 9mm in hand, the figure walked up to the yard where King was barking roughly. One shot pierced the large dog's head, instant entry through the gate into the kitchen was granted. The door was unlocked, and the house alarm did not sound off as the figured poured gas everywhere around the kitchen, all over the counters.

When the figure turned to reveal her face, it was Charity. She began walking through the hall foyer. Leaving the den, she poured gas all over the furniture, on the curtains, the walls and the system. She walked into Trenice's room where she shot Trenice and Diva in their heads. She poured gasoline all over the bed, the whole room. She continued to walk down the hallway into the office; poured gas on the office floor, desk, computer, and bookshelves. As she continued down the hallway to reach the master bedroom, Nicole and I were awakened.

Then, she said, "You haven't told her Tyrone? You haven't told her you're in love with me?" Nicole asked, "What's she talking about?" "I do not know Nicole. She's crazy. I don't love her," I was saying. Then, Charity shot me in the leg. There was no sound. I would have thought the gun would have made a loud sound after the shot.

As I screamed in pain, Nicole screamed, "No! Please don't kill us. You can have whatever you want." Charity said, "Shut up Bitch!" while pointing the gun at Nicole. Nicole blocked her face with her arm as if she could stop the bullet that was going to ricochet through her arm piercing her skull. She never pulled the trigger. Please don't kill my wife. "Tell her then Tyrone!" Charity screamed. "Tell her what happened. Tell her about our affair. Tell her!"

Nicole didn't understand. She just looked at me with those pretty eyes, tears flowing down her face. I began to tell her about our encounter. "I promise Nicole, she blackmailed me. See…"

"You bitch!" Charity screamed at Nicole. "Your second time around fucking someone else's man. I knew about you and Ronelle in high school and Royale. He is my husband. I looked at Nicole and said, "You doing her husband?"

Charity said, "It's best to confess your sins before leaving this earth." Look at you, it hurts doesn't it? My real name is Tameka Bryant, left cheerleader next to you in high school, Ms. Beauty Queen of the prom…And Nicole's eyes got big as four shots hit Nicole in the chest. Tyrone screamed, "NOOOOO! What the fuck have you done you crazy bitch? Why????"

Grabbing Nicole's dead body, "I'm sorry." Charity standing on the side of the bed, "I should've been did this shit. Got her out the way. Now that that's done, I want to fuck before I kill you." Tyrone screamed, "Fuck you! Kill me! Fuck you! Kill me! Fuck you! Kill me!" Charity pointed the gun at him and said, "I'm not going to kill you. I'm going to burn you alive like you are in hell."

As she began to laugh so loud the walls began to shake. Shake so bad the ceiling started caving in, she splashed gas on the bed again and again and again. Charity lit a match and boom. I jumped up screaming "NOOOOOOOO!!!"

Nicole jumped up turning on the lamp, "Baby! Baby! Tyrone!!!" She called. "Are you okay?" I was sitting up in the bed trembling like a wet puppy. I looked over at Nicole. She was fine. The house was quiet. Charity wasn't there. Sweat was dripping from my head as I grabbed Nicole frantically shaking while looking for bullet holes in my wife's chest. I pulled the covers off me to see if my knee was shattered from the bullet. "Everything's okay Baby. You were just having a nightmare. Are you okay?"

"Honey, you were having a nightmare," Nicole comforted me. I sighed. "Baby, I had this terrible nightmare. That crazy lady came in the house. She killed King, Trenice, Diva and You. She burned me alive in the house. It seemed so real, "Baby, I'm here. You see? I'm here."

When Charity came walking into the room with a gun in her hand pointing it at both of us. "It's not a dream. It's reality." A gunshot went off. I screamed jumping out of my sleep but this time not so loud, to wake Nicole. I got up from the bed, sat there for a second. The time read 3:20 a.m. in the morning.

When I got up, I went into the restroom to throw water on my face. "A nightmare," I whispered to myself. A slight smile came across my face in the mirror, but I wasn't smiling. The mirror seemed like it came to life with my reflection and it said you're not dreaming. "This is real. Why did you kill her?"

My reflection began to deform as if the face began to turn into droop. "You killed her," I said as my reflection face peeled off as if it was burning and melting like a candle. The light went off. I ran out of the restroom and instead of me stepping on the carpet of our bedroom, I fell off a cliff or something. I was screaming. It was black, so dark until I couldn't see myself.

I put my hands to my eyes. A light was at the bottom of my fall, but it was taking forever to get to me and where my fall stopped in mid-air.

I was actually looking at the reflection from above. I had fallen to the bottom of darkness. I walked, where I didn't know but I strolled the way of sound. It sounded like a loud waterdrop, a loud flatline sound. I dropped down to my knees and began to I hold my ears.

My heart was beating. I heard bump bump, bump bump, bump bump. I called out, "Is anybody there?" The echo bounced from one end of the darkness to the other end of the darkness. I stopped and noticed a light was coming towards me. "Who's there?" I said and another echo shattered through the dark. The light got closer.

When it went out almost 4 feet away from me and a female laughed but stopped. I started turning and looking around. I was looking for that someone who was carrying the light. When I turned, a face was right in my face and I came up in the air. I could see her. Her face was empty with wet hair in her face dripping as if she was in water. Her eyes popped open fast and wide; her face jumped towards me.

That scared me so bad that I jumped. The lady said, "She killed me, she killed me." I opened my eyes it was my mother-in-law. "Tyrone, she killed me. She used a needle." She started to cry. "She killed me Tyrone." The voice got louder. Then, the lady vanished. I woke up to Nicole shaking me. "Tyrone, Tyrone, Tyrone," she was constantly calling me.

I jumped up for the third time. Three dreams in one night... Nicole asked, "Who killed who Tyrone?" I was in a daze. Nicole asked again, "Who killed who Tyrone?" She was sounding as if she was getting frustrated as if she knew my dream.

I turned to my wife and started telling her about Charity in my dream. Then, the second dream. Then, what the mirror did and when I dropped off a ledge leaving our restroom into a dark black hole. I told Nicole I seen her mother. She was down there Honey. She cried, "She killed me! She killed me!" I couldn't ask her who because she vanished.

Nicole stared at me for a minute. She didn't say nothing. Her eyes were searching my face as if she was thinking on what to say. I apologized, "I'm sorry Honey, but it was true. It was a dream. I'm quite sure that dream was confirmation to who killed her." Nicole said, "Maybe so Honey, but who would want to murder my mother, your mother-in-law? I don't understand. She was just too sweet of an old lady."

Nicole looked as if calling her mom old was not good, I'm sorry but that's what Momma was a little sweet woman. "No," Nicole said. "You said it…little old lady." Not sounding mad "but Baby I didn't mean for you to take it the wrong way. I…" Nicole cut me off. She was exiting the bed and going to the restroom.

"Do you understand?" I asked her. She closed the door. I laid back on my pillow, holding my head. My feet were cold. I looked at the closed restroom door. I was hoping that this time wasn't a dream. So, I pinched myself "Ouch!" Nicole said, "Are you okay Honey?" "Yes Dear," I replied. "Good," I whispered. Not a dream this time. The bed was cold as I got out of it because urine was on the sheets. I thought, "How in the world?" Then, I heard the toilet flush signaling Nicole was getting ready to walk out of the restroom. I ran and opened my underwear drawer, grabbing the first pair of briefs in sight, slipping them on.

As the restroom door opened, "What are you doing Honey?" "Oh, putting on underwear. It was cold." I said as I was slipping my boxers up. Nicole asked if I was up for a cup of coffee? I looked at the clock and it was 3:20 a.m. Again, I squinched in confusion. Nicole was walking through the hallway as she shouted, "I'll turn the AC down." "Okay," I answered in a low tone.

I began pulling the sheets back since they were wet from my mishap as I figured it happened when I was scared in my nightmares. I started pulling the sheets off the bed in a rush to put another fitted and top sheet on to hide my accident. I was moving really fast so I could get the sheets to the washroom. It took me almost 3 minutes to fix the bed back like it was and place the comforter back on the bed.

Then, I went to the washroom to put the sheets into the washer without Nicole realizing I had changed the sheets because I was embarrassed. She shouted from the kitchen, "Honey! You okay?" Not realizing I had entered the kitchen, she jumped. "Baby, you scared me," as she turned around to see me standing there.

"I got a pot of coffee on. You have a seat. Would you like some toast Baby?" as she wrapped her arms around me. "Tyrone, it was just a nightmare, Honey. It's only confirming that your grieving my mother's passing. I promise there's nothing else and maybe Charity was still sitting on your mind from yesterday morning," Nicole said trying to calm me down.

She released her grasp from around my waistline at the sound of the coffee pot buzzer. "Hot coffee," Nicole said softly. She brought a hot pad and the pot to the breakfast bar and sat both things down. As she poured two cups of coffee (Folgers).

"It seemed so real Nicole. I mean right there in view," I continued. Nicole said, "Maybe you need to take a load off by going to the gym Sweetie or maybe you should stay in for today and relax. Put on a nice movie." The clock on the microwave read 4:04 a.m. "Why don't the both of us just finish our coffee and get back into bed?" I wanted to say, "No, it's wet," but I did not because I was still embarrassed.

Nicole stated, "Tameka and Shawna are coming in town today. They are staying at Momma's house so I will go get Trenice and Diva today." I responded with a simple "Oh yeah?" Nicole continued on by saying "They are going to be here until the funeral." "And when did you find out about this Honey?" I asked. Nicole answered, "Yesterday. They are both flying in and Katrina is already here. With all 3 of my sisters around, it will be a blessing. I can use that for now Baby."

As I looked at my wife, I knew she needed her siblings to continue living life. What made matters worse is the warden would not let her brother come home for the funeral.

CHAPTER

8

Tuesday morning, 7:00a.m. Detective Abrams was at it early calling the Tucker's residence. Nicole rolled over after hearing the sound of her cell phone ringing. She reached and grabbed her phone bringing it to her ear. Tyrone was still asleep; she pressed talk.

Nicole started, with a sleepy hello voice, "Detective Abrams, hi." "Good morning Mrs. Tucker. I'm sorry to wake you this early but I think we have a lead on a suspect but before I assume, I have to question. Do you know a Diva Scott?"

Nicole said, "Yes! That's my two-year-old grandbaby. Why?" Nicole asked. "Well, her fingerprints came across our forensic search that showed maybe she touched the closet. "Okay. Mrs. Tucker, I'm sorry to have awakened you but with a case like this you just can't be too sure." "I understand," Nicole agreed.

"Well thank you. Mrs. Tucker?" "I'm still here," Nicole said before hanging up. "Mrs. Tucker," Detective Abrams quickly called. "Yes!" Nicole answered again. "Are you familiar with a Mrs. Linfield?" Abrams asked. Nicole answered, "Yes!" "How do you know her?" Abrams continued. Nicole sat up and asked was she okay? Abrams stated, "Yes. She's fine." And, explained how she had seen someone snooping around her mother's home on Sunday morning.

"Oh my God!" Nicole shouted in surprise. Tyrone raised up. "What's going on Honey?" "Well…" Abrams continued, "I'm going to need Mr.

Tucker and you to come to the station to be present when we bring Mrs. Linfield in for more questioning to see if you can make out who she described as our perpetrator." "Okay," Nicole answered. Then, the two hung up.

Tyrone held Nicole's hand. "What is it Baby?" Nicole started by saying Mrs. Linfield had seen some woman by Momma's house. Tyrone started thinking about his dream and his gut feeling kicked in when he saw his mother-in-law in his dream that told him she killed me. Tyrone shook his head as if he didn't understand when he figured his wife's mother was trying to tell him in his dream.

Then, Charity pulled up on him in the church parking lot. It had seemed weird that she was dressed in all black like she was going to a funeral. "Tyrone," Nicole called his name. I snapped back into my senses as Nicole started, "You okay?" "Yes, Baby. I just went into a deep thought on what my dream might have told me. Your mom was trying to say who killed her."

Nicole stared for a moment after remembering what I had told her. "You said," Nicole stated, "my mom came into your dream and said she killed me, and the detective said Mrs. Linfield saw a woman, Tyrone, snooping around Momma's house Sunday morning. Honey," Nicole said as tears began to form in her eyes, "You also said that Momma was trying to tell you a woman did this to her. We both could not go back to sleep." My wife got out of bed, went to brush her teeth, washed her face and came back to the bedroom opening the closet door.

"I have to know," Nicole said moving fast. As I climbed out of bed, "Do you need me to come with you Honey?" "Yes, I need you to come. The Detective asked for both of us to come to the station," Nicole said. I began to get dressed and remembered that I wet the bed. So, I needed to take a quick shower. I didn't understand, after pinching myself. I even changed the sheets.

I went to the washer and lifted the top. I noticed the sheets in the washer and lifted them. A maybe I was dreaming again imagining me wetting the bed. I smiled from the black hole of my dream, but it was only another image of my imagination.

I walked to the closet, my wife was putting on a pair of tennis shoes, stripping herself of her professional look. I pulled a pair of jogging pants off the top shelf and slipped them on after my shower along with a pair tennis shoes. Then, I went to my side of the bed, opened the T-shirt drawer and pulled out a state fair T-shirt. I slipped into it and grabbed a baseball cap off top the chest of drawers, grabbed my watch, chain and keys. Then I asked Nicole if she was ready.

She said, "Yes." So, we headed out to the truck. I opened the door, pulled out of the garage and proceeded to the station. At 8:30 am, Nicole and I exited the Escalade and headed to the entrance of the station.

I held the door open for my wife as we entered the building and headed towards the receptionist desk. There sat three policewomen behind the desk. Nicole started, "We are here to speak to Detective Abrams."

The female officer replied Detective Abrams is not in at the moment. She should be in at 9:00 am. If you want to wait for her, you can. She is normally on time. "Okay. Thank you," Nicole answered. My wife and I went to have a seat in the chairs along the wall. I looked at the clock on the wall as it read 9:20 am. The detective had not arrived at 9 am, so Nicole called the last number on her received calls list.

"Detective Abrams," she said. "Hello. I was calling to let you know that my husband and I are sitting in the lobby waiting on you." "Oh really?" Detective Abrams replied. "Well, I'll be right down." After they hung up the phone, Nicole looked over at Tyrone who was half asleep. "Honey?" Nicole called out.

I opened my eyes, arms folded, "Yeah," I answered. Don't you know that Detective Abrams has been in that office since we have been here?" "You're kidding," I said. "Nope," Nicole replied back. "Well, why the hell would the officers at the front desk tell us that she was not here? They could have called and let her know that we were here waiting on her."

Nicole gave me the evil eye and said, "You know what? I don't know but I'm going to give her a piece of my mind." I told her, "Nicole, don't go messing with those officers." She didn't listen and she walked straight towards the receptionist desk.

When she got there, she smacked her hand flat on the desk. The female officers just kept on laughing and playing around, so, my wife slapped her hand on the desk again and they all stopped what they were doing and turned towards her.

One of the officers looked at her and asked, "Yes, can we help you?" Nicole replied sharply now, "I just got off the phone with Detective Abrams and she told me that she has been up there in her office ever since we arrived, and you told me that she was not in yet. Why would you lie and have us waiting for no apparent reason?"

The female officer got up and I got up too. I walked over to get my wife and heard the officer tell her "Now look! You need to calm down." Nicole answered back "No. I'm not going to calm down because you work for the citizens, not yourselves. That's the problem." "Sir, get your wife before she ends up in jail." The other female cop spoke as on lookers passed by. "No, I'm not going to nobody's jail," Nicole said. The other two officers walked around the counter and the first officer was going word for word with Nicole.

Detective Abrams walked up, "Now! Now! Now Ladies! It's ok. It's early in the morning and we are all stressing. Nicole said, "She told me that you weren't in the office which caused my husband and I to just sit down here waiting for you while they skinned, grinned and laughed (saying ha ha ha) in each other's faces while there is a murderer on the loose."

Detective Abrams calmed down the officers and asked Nicole and I to "come this way". The two officers went back behind the desk. As the three of us went up the escalator, my wife was so upset I could see the veins running down the center of her forehead.

As we reached the top of the escalator, the state-of-the-art police department was nice with big plants everywhere. There were plaques of police that retired, promoted or died in the line of fire while on duty hung on the wall, the president, Barack Obama, was on the wall along with President John F. Kennedy.

Detective Abrams closed the door behind us as we arrived and entered her office. "Take a seat," she offered. Then, she walked behind her desk and sat down. She had pictures all over the office including family portraits. It smelled like it belonged to a woman as the scents of tropical fruit were lingering in the air.

Now, Detective Abrams started, "We got the fingerprints back. They only indicate family as having been in the house. They happened to belong to you, Mrs. Tucker, which does not make you a suspect. We do not believe that you would murder your own mother. We also found prints from your mother and Diva Scott, but there is one concern. We found some footprints on the side of the house at her bedroom window.

It looks to be a size 7 1/2 in women's shoes plus a handprint on the outside of the window which we could not pull. We are definitely considering a small woman as a suspect." I noticed my wife's eyes fill with tears. The detective continued, "but we have no prints on the woman. We also found a bottle of morphine and some knock out medicine. A handkerchief was also found under the bed along with a syringe cap to a needle.

I'm thinking that the footprints that lead from outside the bedroom window belonged to the suspect who climbed through the window and hid in the closet. We found footprints there as well. We further believe that the suspect hid in the closet and waited for your mother to fall asleep. Once she was asleep, the woman poured the knockout medicine into the handkerchief, came out of the closet and pressed the hanky around her face." Nicole began to muffle as if she could not hold it in.

The detective stopped as she passed Nicole some tissue, "I'm sorry Mrs Tucker. I know this can be quite difficult to handle. Our evidence leads us to believe..." "It's ok," Nicole said in a low whisper looking down. I grabbed my wife's hand and began to rub and rub. "It's okay Honey. It's ok," I said.

The detective started again. "Now, this is why we wanted the two of you to come here." She didn't finish describing what they believed had happened due to the emotional effect it was having on my wife. "So, Mrs. Linfield should be here any moment. We will interrogate her for further details, and we will have a sketch artist in the observation with you two sketching a drawing to see who we are looking for as a suspect. Then, maybe we can put a name on our Jane Doe. Okay?" Detective Abrams' desk phone rang. She picked up, "Detective Abrams. Okay. Can you walk her up? I'm with two clients now. Thank you."

As she hung up the receiver, she said, "That was the receptionist downstairs." A serious look came across Nicole's face, Detective Abrams smiled which made Nicole smile. Then I smiled.

"I know," Abrams said, "those women were probably being lazy." Nicole stated, "Right because all they had to do was call your extension and we could have been up here. "Well, Mrs. Tucker," Abrams added, "they know next time not to play around with you, plus they probably were jealous of you."

"Well," Nicole said. "Yes!" Abrams said. "I don't know why. Look how I'm dressed." "They probably like your man." Nicole looked around at me to catch me grinning as I stopped immediately. "Well, they're definitely looking for problems," she said further. Abrams interrupted, "Hey! Look, I'm going to escort the two of you to the observation area where you will be seating and fetch the sketcher so we can get this show on the road. Okay? Follow me."

I had this crazy thought in my head… "What if my mother-in-law's murderer is Charity?" As I shook my head "No!" We walked out the office. Other detectives greeted Abrams as we walked down the hall to the right. When we walked in there were two detectives sitting in the room with coffee mugs on the table, looking through a glass. On the other side was Mrs. Linfield.

"Hey guys," Abrams greeted the two and then introduced us to them. "Detective Watts, this is Mr. & Mrs. Tucker." He reached to shake our hands. "And this is Detective Jones. He's one of our greatest detectives in all of Texas," Abrams continued. "Hey!" Detective Watts said in jealousy. "I suck too," he joked "…coffee mugs," Detective Jones joked back. "Well Abrams, what you got?" Jones asked.

"Well, Mrs. Tucker's mother was murdered Sunday morning." "I'm so sorry to hear that. What kind of lead do we have?" Jones asked. "Well, we only have this sweet lady to describe to us how the actual suspect looked," Abrams announced.

"You mean to tell me she saw the suspect?" Watts exploded. Abrams nodded her head "Yes." "Wow, this will be great. I'm waiting on Jimmy. You need Jim. He's great at sketching." Jones looked over at me and said, "You are going to love this guy." Watts asked, "Well, why is the old lady sitting in the questioning booth?" Abrams stated, "Because Mrs.

Linfield happened to be a close friend of the family and we don't need her distracted if she happens to see Mrs. Tucker."

"Ooh," Watts replied as he began to understand Abrams logic. "See why I'm the best?" Detective Jones reached out and Watts balled up his fist. "Assault and battery," Jones jokingly said. Nicole and I smiled. "So, okay. Where's Jimmie?

As the door opened, "Here I am." A short half bald old white guy walked into the room. "Here I am. I'm coming. "This can be all day," I figured after looking at this guy. He didn't look like who they expected him to be. "Okay move aside you donut eaters," Jimmy said as he was speaking about Jones & Watts. He set his pack of pencils and a clear white sketch pad on the table while placing his electric pencil sharpener on the table and plugged it into the wall.

Watts laughed at the body motion of the little man. He looked to be 3 ft tall like an ancient Elf of Santa Clause and he had a coffee mug snapped to a strap on his belt. As he unstrapped the cup and strolled over to the coffee pot, he said "Get out of my way, Free Willie!" Jones laughed at Watts saying, "He does look like Free Willie, doesn't he?" Detective Abrams chuckled.

As she introduced little Jimmie to us, "Jimmie, this is Mr. & Mrs. Tucker. They are the ones you are going to be helping today." He looked up with his big bifocals on his little head and said, "Oh yeah? I didn't notice you." Watts laughed, "What's funny Pork Fat?"

As the rest of us laughed at the joke Jimmie snuck in on Watts, he walked over to Nicole. "Hi Mrs. Lady. You're such a beauty and who is this guy?" I stated to him, "Mr. Tucker." I know that Jimmie attacked me. "What's a beautiful lady like yourself doing with a razorback like him? "Now now," I said.

"I'm just kidding Kong Zilla," Jimmie said waving me off. Nicole laughed, "Ahh, that's my husband." "Wow! You are not so lucky." Nicole laughed again, as I stood there in agony, but it was ok. I see he was the laughter of the stock.

"Now, what we got?" Jimmie asked. "Well, Detective Abrams started, "that lady in there will describe our suspect and you are going to sketch what she describes." Jimmie looked at Mrs. Linfield, "She's a beauty. Where you get her?" Nicole said, "She's a friend of the family."

Jimmie looked at Mrs. Linfield as if he fell in love with her. "Okay Detective Abrams, since I'm doing you a favor, when I get done, I want you to introduce us." Nicole started to say something but second guessed it. "Okay," Detective Abrams said, "let's get started."

As Detective Abrams went into the room, Jimmie put on his earphones while sipping a cup of coffee. I could hear Detective Abrams talking to Mrs. Linfield, "Hi Mrs. Linfield. I'm sorry that this is taking so much time. Did you want a cup of coffee or something?" Mrs. Linfield said, "No." Detective Abrams stated, "At any time you decide, you do you can stop this, and we will get it. Mrs. Linfield tell me about Sunday morning. Tell me about the woman you saw around you friend's, Mrs. Harris, house."

Detective Abrams pulled out a note pad. "Well Detective, I was sitting in my recliner like I always do. My blinds and curtains are always open so I can see out in front of my house. Plus, my plants need the sunlight. I saw an SUV pull up and a lady exited the truck." "How tall did she look?" Abrams interrupted. Mrs. Linfield said, "A little bit of 5ft." "Okay," Abrams wrote down. "Such a short woman," Mrs. Linfield stated.

"What did her face look like?" "She had on sunshades," Mrs. Linfield reported. As she continued, Jimmie began to sketch. The detective resumed questioning, "How did her face look in build? Was it skinny, medium, round?"

Mrs. Linfield said it was a medium round face build. "How did her hair appear?" Detective Abrams asked. "Short, not past her earlobes," Mrs. Linfield. "Was her hair curly, long, or straight Mrs. Linfield?" She said, "Oh, she had long hair shoulder length." "Yes," the detective continued. Mrs. Linfield asked how Nicole was doing because she hadn't seen her since her mom passed away.

"I feel so sorry for that poor child. She was the only child to keep up with her mom. All the others moved away." Mrs. Linfield explained Nicole's family story. "How nice," Abrams commented. "Was she dark skinned, brown skinned, a white lady or what?"

"She had golden brown skin and she had on all black too," Mrs. Linfield continued. Detective Abrams further asked, "Was there anything particular about this woman that stood out to you?" Mrs.

Linfield looked up as if she was trying to remember what she saw. "Oh," Mrs. Linfield remembered her earrings were long and dangling with a necklace around her neck. "What color hair did she have?" Abrams continued to ask.

"Her hair was black in color." "Okay, Mrs. Linfield. Give me just a second; I will be back with you." "Okay," Mrs. Linfield answered. "Do you want that cup of coffee now?" Mrs. Linfield said, "Yes, but no sugar. Okay? No cream either." Detective Abrams said coming up as she went through the doors leaving the little old lady sitting there.

Jimmie watched her. His sketch was marvelous. He handed it to Detective Abrams. She walked over to the table and showed me and my wife. My eyes got big because it was Charity; she was right there with the dark shades on. I couldn't believe my eyes. Nicole was thrilled that the sketch was 100% accurate.

"Do you know this woman?" "Yes," Nicole stated. "You, Mr. Tucker?" "Yes, she was at our house on Monday morning for an insurance interview," Nicole stated. She continued, "I had her fill out an application so we could become business partners." "Really?" Detective Abrams said.

"Okay. I need that application so we can move alone with this case and get her off the streets," the detective concluded. "When can you have that information for me?" Detective Abrams asked. "As soon as we get home," we both said in unison. Detective Abrams wanted to know "can you fax it over to us to make this quicker the faster the better?" "Yes, I can fax it over," Nicole stated.

I knew this was getting ready to come to an end and she was going to spill the beans about our connection with what happened last week. I really don't want her to get away with this, but I also don't want her to get me in a jam with my wife and with my marriage with everything that was going on now. It would devastate my wife to know after all this time I had an affair with this woman; the same woman who murdered her mom.

I could feel my throat getting lumps in it really fast. I didn't know what to do. I could only do one thing; I needed to let Charity know that the cops were on to her. Plus, I needed to get to her before they did. Charity hasn't called me back since we met up at Applebee's. I didn't think I would wish that she would call me now so I could warn her, and I needed to meet up with her.

I could go over to her house, but the police will probably beat me there. Detective Abrams let us leave to take care of the business she needed done to get in contact with Charity. The whole ride back home Nicole was mainly questioning "why would Charity do such a thing??? She was that upset behind my prices??"

I was in deep thought if I could get hold of the paperwork first, but Nicole's mindset was on getting the paperwork over to the detective immediately. Mrs. Linfield saw Charity; that was the same dress she wore to church when we saw her. Nicole was on the phone. Her sister was in town and waiting for us to arrive.

Nicole began to get more emotional about the situation. I couldn't stand to see my wife this way. I couldn't even stand to see her knowing about my affair with this woman; if I go on and tell her she would be destroyed. As we turned onto our street, her sister was waiting for us. I pulled up into the driveway, her sisters exited the Mercedes Benz that was waiting on us.

Nicole jumped out the truck and the four were reunited. As they hug, all of them were crying, mourning their loss. While they were doing that, I went into the house and went into the office looking for the application. "There it is!" I whispered. I balled it up and placed it into my pocket and rushed right out to the garage. My phone rang and I hurried to answer it…

"Hello." It was Troy. "What up Tee?" He wanted to know if I was at the house. I thought to tell him no but yes came out. I'm at home, he and Monica were coming over to pay their respects to Nicole. I told him they were more than welcome to do so.

Nicole, Katrina, Tameka, and Shawna were still standing as they all had tears in their eyes, Nicole was telling her three sisters where she just came from and what we just discovered Katrina could not believe what she was hearing then she exploded the same bitch that came to your house was the one that murdered Momma? I will kill that slut where she lives. The police better make it there before I do, which reminded Nicole of the document she needed to fax over to Detective Abrams. Nicole walked off inviting her three sisters inside. The three sisters followed as

Katrina was still hot about finding out Charity killed her momma, but she went on inside.

I was a little comfortable about the situation for the time being as I went into the house where all the women were, Nicole was in her office searching for the application Nicole began to search her files, nothing, as I walked into the office, she said that she thought she grabbed it during the course of our disagreement. Nicole gave a suspicious look at me as if she couldn't remember.

I'm thinking about her having that disagreement when Katrina runs in causing more commotion. As she turned to grab the application and stormed out of the house, "No!" Nicole said, "because when all of it was over, I remember putting it there" while she was pointing at a stack of other applications "and typing it into the computer."

"Oh, I didn't get as far as her name and address is when I stopped, she started complaining about the prices," Nicole continued. "Okay," I said. My heart began to race as if she still had the information in the computer. I began to worry as I watched her log into her accounts by using the client's name and there it was…Charity Hunter and all the rest of her information pulled up.

I can remember her address. It was 1217 Wind Brook Lane but the address she gave was 1101 Wind Chester Dr. which I knew wasn't true. So, that gave me enough time to get Charity first before the cops grabbed her. Nicole began to print the information. That's when the doorbell ring and I heard Tameka answer the door.

As the door opened, the buzzer beeped, and a lot of commotion was going on which let me know that Troy and Monica had made it over. I started to the front of the house. All of them were sitting in the den. "Hey Troy! What's going on? Hey Monica," as I reached out to give her a hug.

Monica asked for Nicole, "Oh she's in the office." "Okay, strong lady at work still?" "Nah, taking care of something." That's when Nicole walked into the den too. Monica immediately began crying and running towards her.

"I'm sorry Girl" as the two held each other crying. I told Troy to come and see what I had. As we passed the two ladies, I began telling Troy everything about Mrs. Linfield, about the sketch and all. Troy couldn't believe it. He was like, "What are you thinking about doing?" "Man, at a time like this," I said, "I just can't come out with the truth right now. That's going to crush her whole world man."

Troy said, "I know what…This is what we are going to do. We need to go to her house. I'll think of something when we get there but don't the police have her information?" Troy asked. "Well, no," I said. "The address I followed her to was not the same address she put on her application."

"Okay but once the detectives find out about the false address, they may find out about her real one. So, we have to get a move on it," Troy explained. So, the two of us left the house and started heading over to Charity's residence.

"What are we going to do once we get there?" Troy said. "I don't know," I answered, "but we need to keep her from getting caught by the police. She could ruin my marriage man," I stated as I drove the truck as fast as I could. Then, my phone rang, "Hello, Troy with you?" Nicole asked. "Yes!" I answered. "Where are you both going?" Nicole asked.

"To the beer store. We will be right back," I said. "Okay," Nicole said before hanging up. "That was Nicole," both of us said it at the same time. I laughed because he already knew who it was on the phone.

Ten minutes later, we pulled up to Charity's residence but around the corner of her house. There was a car in the driveway. We got out and Troy began to whistle to see if they had a dog in the yard. As we went around the house, the back door was open. I grabbed the door handle of the house and we both went inside.

"Nobody seemed to be home," I whispered. I could hear a television on as a little girl began to laugh. "Oh shit!" Troy whispered, "Someone is here." I put my finger on my lips to signal for him to be quiet. I heard her talking as if she was on the phone. As we crept around the kitchen to the hallway, the room door was closed where the voice was coming from; the house seemed to have four rooms. I didn't know which room was which.

I whispered to Troy, "Find a closet. Then, when Charity comes home, we are going to grab her; put a bag over her head and kidnap her." Troy said, "Are you crazy" with a low whisper. The girl hung up the phone and Troy ran into the closet. I ran into another room to take cover.

The girl came out of her room as you can hear her walking through the house, she opened the front door and left the house, Troy didn't move I came out the room to see if she was gone. I ran into the front room and peeped through the blinds. The young girl was walking up the street going over to a friend's house.

"Good," I said. Troy responded, "She's gone." He came out the closet saying, "Hey man, we can't do this. This is wrong! She's going to have us locked up. This is trespassing & burglary." "Okay," I replied. "I have never been to jail," Troy continued. "Shut up Troy!" I almost yelled. "This is going to work.

All we have to do is grab her, duct tape her mouth and her hands, and be out. Troy didn't seem like he was down with none of this. I told him, "Man, find some tape around here." Troy looked in the kitchen, I looked in the closet. Then the bathroom. Troy yelled, "I found some!" "Good!" I said. Then, we heard a car pulling up.

Troy ran into the back and said, "Someone is here." "Man," I told him to hide. The front door opened, Troy ran into the closet and I ran into the backroom. A lady's voice filled the air of the quiet house. I started to think about the little girl that just left the house. Wasn't she supposed to be in school? Then, it hit me…"Ooh! She's cutting. That's why the back door was open."

As Charity was walking through the house, she started singing. She opened the refrigerator door, then closed it. She walked into the room where I was hiding and started talking to herself saying "Damn, I'm fine" while laughing at herself.

I laid under the bed. She dropped her dress, pulled off her heels and then her bra dropped to the floor. She went into the restroom and turned on the shower. The shower door opened, then closed. I slid from under the bed and called for Troy. "Hey Troy," I whispered again. He came out the closet. "Okay, she's in the shower," I told him. Let's grab her right when she gets out the shower. You get behind the door. I'm going to drop her phone onto the floor so she can bend down and grab it. Once she does then that's when I'm going to grab her.

"Okay," Troy said. Troy got into position and I grabbed her phone and pressed the volume. It rung constantly as I got beside the dresser and dropped her phone on the floor. The shower door opened, and Charity came running out to her phone. She spotted it on the floor. When she bent down to pick her phone up, Troy grabbed her from behind.

She began to kick and scream as I ran over putting the duct tape on her mouth and hands, then her feet. I also placed a pillowcase on her head. She was squirming like a worm as I took the duct tape and went around the bottom of the pillowcase to keep it from coming off her head. She kicked and kicked.

Troy said, "Damn, she's fine." Then, I said, "How are we going to get her out of the house?" Now that she's all duct taped up; Troy looked as if he was nervous. She squirmed and squirmed then the front door opened.

We both looked at each other "Oh shit!" Thinking it was her daughter, but we heard a man shout, "Honey!" Then, we both tipped to the back room. I hid behind the door, Troy went into the bathroom and turned off the light. We left Charity there on the floor squirming. When he walked into the room, he noticed her legs hanging out from the front of the bed.

As he rushed over, Troy ran from the bathroom and tackled him which looked like something from the NFL. The two guys flipped over the nightstand. I ran over to help Troy. The guy didn't have a chance with the two of us. He tried to pick up the lamp. I threw him a punch which hit him directly in his jaw. Troy had his arms when his shirt raised up; he had a gun.

I grabbed the gun and pointed it at him and said, "Okay. Enough is enough." Troy let go of him. I cocked the gun back and the guy stood straight up with his hands raised into the air saying, "Okay. You got me. Whatever you want you can have it. Take it. Just don't kill me."

When I realized what I was doing, I had just become a criminal, doing a criminal act. The black guy stood at least 6 ft 4 inches and looked to be in his mid-40's. Then he stated, "I know you. You're Nicole's husband." Charity stopped squirming as she started listening.

"Man, I didn't do it. She came onto me Man," the guy was trying to reason with me. What I had just heard traumatized me. I began to shake, and the guy realized I was really angry. He started to try and calm me down by saying, "Calm down Man. Don't kill me. I wasn't wrong. She wanted me, not me wanting her," he continued.

I asked him, "What the hell are you talking about?" As I looked down scratching my head, I blanked out. Then, Troy grabbed him. I thought he was trying to shoot him. On accident, he fell to the floor after taking he bullet. Charity started to squirm as if she was trying to get away from us.

The shot was so loud I just knew the neighbors had heard it. As I panicked, Troy panicked too. He said, "What the fuck did you just do man?" Troy said, "This plan is all fucked up Man. You have gone crazy." "Hey! You saw him. I thought he was trying to attack you," I said to him. Troy said, "No Man. I grabbed him to get ready and duct tape him up." Tyrone said, "Man, I blanked out for a moment. I thought he was trying to attack you man." "Shit!" Troy cried out, "Fuck man!" Troy screamed.

Charity was still squirming in a frantic state not knowing if she was next to get shot. I looked at her and Troy said, "Man, let's get the fuck out of here! Man, we need to get the fuck out of here Tyrone," Troy said again. I just stood there in a daze. "Tyrone!" Troy screamed. "Let's go!" "What about her?" I asked. "Fuck her Man! We got to go!" Troy said impatiently. Troy yelled desperately, "Man, just give me the key. I'm going to get the fuck out of here."

Troy grabbed my pocket for the keys, and I knocked his hand away. "Tyrone, Man, don't do this shit! Man let's go!" I said, "We can't just leave. She knows who we are, and she heard everything Man. If we leave her alive, she's going to tell the police everything about what happened. I'm ruined. I'm going to lose my wife, my job, my house, my family. I got too much to lose Man." Troy ran out the room.

I removed the duct tape from around the pillowcase Charity had tears in her eyes as I removed the duct tape off her mouth. She gasped for air. "Please," she started, "Tyrone, don't do this to me. My daughter needs me. Don't kill me." She pleaded for her life. I looked at Charity and I said, "I have no choice."

Charity began to cry frantically saying, "I don't want to die Tyrone. I'm sorry for everything. I wasn't going to call you anymore. I was going to leave you alone. Tyrone please don't kill me. Please! Please!"

She cried and tears came into my eyes as I stood over her. She screamed so loudly that it hurt my eardrums. Then, I let two shots off into her head and turned around and let another shot off in the back of the guy's head. Then, I left the house. When I made it to the truck, Troy was leaning on the hood with tears in his eyes and I said, "All of those shots and no one came out of their house?" Troy looked at me and said man take me to my wife.

I looked at Troy and said, "Man, I'm sorry Troy. I didn't mean for none of this to happen. She heard us and she knew who we were." Troy walked passed me with no remark; just ignored me. We both got into the vehicle and pulled off. The whole ride was silent. The whole time, we both were in a daze.

The closer we got to my house, the longer it seemed for us to get there. Finally, we pulled into the driveway. I told Troy again, "Man, I'm sorry." He said, "Done Tyrone. We are not going to get away with this. Tyrone her daughter is going to come back home, see her parents dead in their home and call the police. They are going to investigate; going to come and grab the both of us. Man, the only thing we can do is tell the truth. Tell them what happened."

"Man, we know the truth, but will the courts see it like that? No!" Tyrone said. The ladies were standing outside. "Now, we have to explain why we have all this blood on us," Troy said. "This is going to crush Monica," he said, and I said, "This is going to destroy Nicole." Troy got out all the smiles turned to frowns when they saw Troy's shirt.

Nicole looked right at me as I began to break down. She ran to the truck around on the driver's side and asked what happened. She began to cry. Tyrone what did you do?" "I'm sorry Baby," I stuttered. "I killed her. I killed her and her husband." Nicole asked, "What are you talking about?"

All the women ran to the truck to listen to what I had to say. They all were crying. The sight of five beautiful women crying over the mistake I had made just touched me even more. I wanted to kill myself right there. I put the gun to my head.

Nicole screamed, "No, Tyrone!" As she grabbed my arm, "No, Baby! No don't do this. Please come in the house." Neighbors heard the commotion and began to come outside as I exited the truck and went into the house. We closed the garage door, locked the truck, went inside and sat on the sofa in the den. "Baby let's go into the room. Come talk to me Honey. Please talk to me." As I got up, Nicole told everyone to excuse us and we went into our room.

Nicole closed the door and hugged me so tightly. She cried and cried and cried. I just don't understand why all of this is happening to us. Why is it happening to us like this? I looked at Nicole and I started to tell her, "Baby, I knew who you were dealing with." She looked at me and she told me to continue. "I found out about you and his affair. He knew your name."

Nicole stated that she was sorry, and she told me about him. She started saying, "He was a client and one thing lead to another. It just happened." I told her I was hiding something myself. Then, I told her all about Charity and her blackmailing me on several occasions. I told her I thought he was trying to hurt Troy. Then, the gun went off, shooting him.

I was going to kidnap Charity so the cops wouldn't get her, and she wouldn't expose our affair. I was afraid of losing you Honey. I'm sorry Baby. I didn't want this to happen like this. I always wanted it to be just you and me; I never cheated on you Nicole. She blackmailed her way in my life. She wanted to get even with her husband; she knew about you and him. I never knew until now. Nicole just stood there and listened. She was so in shock. I grabbed my woman and walked her over to the bed, put the gun on the nightstand as the two of us climbed into the bed, holding each other. I laid there thinking it's not going to be long before the cops come in my house to get me and arrest me, hours passed we were still lying in the bed. Nobody came to disturb us.

CHAPTER

9

Police cars were everywhere at 1217 Wind Brook Lane. The coroners were rolling two bodies out in body bags to transport them to the morgue for further investigations. Forensic scientists were all over the house, finger printing everything in sight. Detective Jones and Watts were at the scene too taking notes. Detective Jones said, "The forensics are on it now." As he hung up his cell phone, "We should know by the end of the day on everything that comes back." He was telling Watts the news will air live at 6:00 p.m.

Nicole and I was still lying in the bed getting in our last moments together. The news lady was beginning, "Hi. My name is Paula Ross, Channel 8 News. There was a double homicide committed today around 10:00 a.m. According to the police report, the daughter of both victims came home to find her parents murdered.

The detectives don't have anything to go on right now at this moment. I will have the latest news at 12 O'clock. My name is Paula Ross signing out at your local News 8. I felt my life was ruined. I let my wife down...my family. I started thinking about how hard I tried to keep my kids from struggling and making the right decisions in life. My foundation I built for my kids and my wife.

I'm done. Nicole's sisters were still in the living area hanging around to make sure everything was okay. Nicole was lying on my chest when the phone began to ring. Nicole's phone has been ringing every 30 minutes; she never picked up. I had turned my phone off. I couldn't sleep or nap because so much was going through my head at the time. It was so confusing to even think.

Nicole was getting ready to make a phone call when her phone started ringing again. It read "City Phone." Nicole answered, "Hello." "Hi, Nicole Tucker." A man's voice came across the receiver. "Yes," my wife answered.

"Hi. My name is Detective Jones. I believe we met this morning. Detective Abrams spoke with you and your husband Mrs. Tucker." "Yes!" "Well, I have been trying to reach you to inform you that we did find that suspect who murdered your Momma but I'm sorry to tell you she's dead," the detective announced.

"Is your husband anywhere around?" Nicole hesitated but she said yes. As she handed the phone over to me, I said "Hello", but my words were trapped inside of my vocal cord. Nothing came out. Then, the detective said, "Mr. Tucker." I said, "Hello" again. Detective Jones came across the receiver and said, "Well, today you and your wife came to the department to identify a suspect. The same suspect that we found today. Both her and her husband shot twice in the head and in the abdomen. Do you know anything about this?" His words echoed.

When he finished, it felt like the world got quiet. Like the spotlight was on me. Everything seemed as like it came crashing down on me. Before I realized it, a big fat lie came out, "No, I don't know anything about it." Nicole looked at me like she was disappointed in me because she wanted me to tell the truth.

I had just made the situation worse because if I didn't know, how did they know to call me and ask specifically for me. If the cops are calling me, they must know.

The detective asked another question…"Do you know Troy Sage?" I didn't say anything. "Look Mr. Tucker, let me cut to the chase. We found yours and Mr. Sage's prints all over the residence. They were everywhere. So, you tell me what I don't know. Look Mr. Tucker I know what you're going through but if you are not going to let me help you, then you are going to make my job harder.

I am personally going to come to get you Mr. Tucker. I'm sorry for all the grief that you and your family have endured. I'll be in touch,"

Detective Jones said. As he hung up, Nicole started, "Tyrone, why did you lie? You should've known the cops would find out. Why do you think they were calling you, Tyrone."

"I know, Nicole, shit! You keep saying this. Nicole sit back. I'm sorry Baby but I don't want to leave you Baby. I got nervous. I thought he was trying to attack Troy and me. I had taken his gun when I thought the guy was trying to attack Troy. My reflexes were to shoot him immediately. Charity was tied up. Troy and I was calling out each other's names. So, I felt since the guy was dead already, I couldn't let Charity live to tell it on us. I was just trying to protect our marriage.

Baby, I'm sorry. I messed up badly. Out of all the years we shared, nothing came between us. I allowed this thing to destroy our marriage. Honey, I wish I could turn back the hands of time. I would go back to that night at the gas station. I would have kept going or called somebody else to help her.

My phone rang. I hesitated at first. Then, I picked up the phone. "Hello," I said. It was Troy. "Did they call you?" Troy asked. "Yes, they just called plus they threaten to come and pick me up," I said.

"So, what now?" Troy asked. "You dragged me into this now drag me out of this Tyrone. The plan you came up with was fucked up. Tyrone, you got to let them know what happened man, all the way from the beginning to the end. Tyrone, you got to tell them how I got involved." So, I said, "You got it Troy."

He said, "Man, you're my friend since college and I got nothing but love for you, but this right here is too much. This thing went too far. I hate this happen and I don't regret helping you either I just can't take no murder rap man."

He asked how my wife was doing. I said, "She's not doing good. She's hurting man." "You really weren't thinking at all." I replied, "I just wanted to protect my marriage and hope that my secret never came out, but it did along with other stuff…Help us Jesus!" Troy didn't say anything. I guess I have to do what's right. Troy started by saying, "Hey! Look at it like this…You got a strong family."

Then, the doorbell rang. My heart started beating fast. Nicole turned and looked at me. Then, she heard her sister answer the door. So, I told Troy, "Let me call you later." So, we both hung up.

As Nicole and I got out of bed, a lady was standing in the den. I could hear her from the hallway. Nicole and I walked to the front of the house. She was asking questions and Katrina was trying to put the lady out and close the door. The lady was still asking questions when Nicole and I made it to the den. It was a reporter. "A reporter I shouted!" Tameka and Shawna looked at me funny. There were more in the front of the house too. I, then, asked Katrina and Shawna for the remote control. I turned the T.V. on the news channel. My wife's face lit up.

"They found our residence but how?" Nicole stated. "They are not supposed to do that," Tameka said as she got up. She ran towards the front door. "Tameka," I yelled, "No! don't go out there!" "No, Tyrone! they are not supposed to do this. What if someone wanted to retaliate for the murder" they know where you live now! She had a point, I thought.

So, Nicole, Katrina, Tameka and Shawna walked out the door. They had reporters everywhere; two News 8 vans, one News 4 van, and one News 11 van. They even had a Spanish News van out there. I'm finished.

My phone started ringing again. "Hello," I answered. It was another friend of the family, the Hendersons, "Tell me it's not true." As I hung up on that person, I knew this was becoming public. I could see it. It won't be long before the detective was going to have me in custody with all this commotion. And I knew it wouldn't be long before the police arrived at my house. King was barking loudly at the strange lights, cameras and reporters as well as the on lookers.

This was so embarrassing to my family as my neighbors were out looking too. They knew what was going on. Now, the police were beginning to pull up. Nicole came back inside. Trenice was on the phone with Nicole crying, wondering what was going on and why this was happening. My son never called. I guess the side of town he was in had not heard or seen the news just yet, but I knew Trenice; she was going to call her brother, not knowing he had not called yet.

I knew that it would not be long before they started calling, trying to figure out what was happening. Also, I knew my boss knew what was happening when he called. All I could say was "I'm sorry" and hung up. Then, I peeped out the door. When Nicole came rushing in, I could see at least three cops pulling up.

I couldn't believe my eyes. I ran to the back of the house towards my room to get the gun and ran to the yard where King was put the gun in the doghouse. I took the clip out of the gun and bullets out the chamber; then I went back inside. King thought it was play time as he ran beside me. I ran to the door and closed it when I got to the end of the hallway by the den. Detective Jones and Watts were already standing in our den area. "Hey Mr. Tucker!" What's going on?" the detective asked as I stopped in my tracks.

He asked me to come over to him. "What's going on Mr. Tucker? I know you have been through a lot over the week and I think it's ok if we don't put you in handcuffs. Let's do it like this. I don't think you will run. We're just going to walk out to the burgundy police cruiser with the tinted windows. You can wave at the cameras. You don't have to answers any questions from the reporters. It's best that you don't but you know your rights."

Nicole was crying and Katrina, Tameka and Shawna were standing around with tears in their eyes. I said nothing. I was just in a daze. Detective Watts started reading me my rights... "You have the right to remain silent. Anything you say or do can be held against you in a court of law. You have the right to an attorney. If you can't afford one, one will be appointed to you. Do you understand your rights?"

As Detective Jones opened the door, cameras were flashing everywhere, reporters flooded my front lawn, and I could hear King barking roughly. I mean he was really barking harshly. Detective Jones was walking on the side of me and Detective Watts walking behind me when I made it to the burgundy cruiser.

Detective Jones opened the door, and the cameras were still flashing. As I looked from behind the tinted windows, my wife's face was hidden into her sister, Tameka's, chest. It hurt me so bad to see my wife in this condition. She lost her Momma, and she lost her husband in the past week or so.

I was trying to protect my marriage but never tried to protect myself. Now that it was over, I realized all I had to do was tell my wife the truth and none of this would be happening. Arraignment court was already awaiting my arrival. My case hit high profile as the detectives walked me in. The judge sat behind the podium and welcomed me. "How are you Mr. Tucker? I'm going to go on and let you know we're charging you with 2 counts of Retaliation Capitol Murder. Your bond will be set at 2 million dollars. Are you going to need the court to appoint you a lawyer?" "No Sir," I stated and that's how I got locked up.

Troy was brought in the next day I heard from my wife. Monica had told her. I never wanted it to go this far. My wife buried her momma 2 days after I was arrested. My son was getting ready to graduate from college soon, and the baby was due in February. It's been 7 months now that I have been locked up. As I lay in my 3x8 foot one man cell, peering from my jail issued blanket, I counted the bricks for almost one hundred times.

There were almost 705 bricks to be exact, in front of me: two square 1/2 inch thick coated with plastic glass panels. It was maybe 4 a.m. and I still can't believe I let this happen to me. How could I let myself fall into a place like this? Trial was getting ready to start today. My lawyer had been back and forth to the jailhouse for the last seven months; he was telling me the D.A. is offering 25 to life, but I could not see that happening. Twenty-five years was not a good offer. I didn't have a criminal record. I had finished college with a 4.0 grade point average, and I was the best tradesman on the site crew of which I had worked.

My financial account was good; I mean great. My character of witness was extremely good. I had a great attendance record with the church and with all that said none of it matters, but faith was the only thing that mattered in this kind of situation: two people dead, mother-in-law passed. So much stood out for my lawyer to argue on.

Troy was charged with two counts of kidnapping and one count of Capitol Murder. His bond was set at 1.7 million dollars. He was able to bond out, but it nearly broke him to do so. But for the last 7 months, he was fighting his case outside. When I walked into the courtroom on trial day, my family, my boss, my pastor, my neighbors, my church members, friends, co-workers were all there to support me. The families of both victims were in the court on the other side too. The judge came in and the bailiff shouted, "All rise!"

As everyone in the court room stood up, "the Honorable Judge Katie Fisk is presiding and you all can be seated," the bailiff concluded. The case reporting lasted over two hours. As the D.A. began his side arguments, my lawyer stuck it back. It was like right and wrong was very mutual in this case. The jury went to lunch and came back; then, the jury left again but this time they had to conclude my case.

The judge put the court in recess. Everyone were talking amongst themselves as I sat and prayed to God the whole time they were out. I said, "Lord, my Father. You know my heart. You knew my only intention was to protect the love of my life and if I was wrong Father, I'm prepared to take whatever you see fit in this situation. I'm giving this to you Lord. In Jesus' name..." Before I could finish my prayer, I heard a voice say "All rise!"

The judge was coming back from her chambers and the jury was already back from deliberation. Everyone sat down. The judge asked the jury did they reach their verdict. A tall black man stood up; his voice sounded as if they had found me guilty. The judge had me to stand. They scheduled my trial first. Troy's trial was set for another date. The jury read "Guilty of all charges!"

My family cried out loudly. They all broke down in the courthouse; family and friends, co-workers and all. The judge shook her head as she had no choice but to sentence me to two life sentences without the possible chance of parole.

I stood there and smiled; I knew that God was only doing his job. I prayed and I put it in his hands. The judge asked me did I have any last words before I was taken away, I stood there with a proud look on my face. I turned to the courts and said, "First, I want to apologize to the victims' families. I didn't want it to go this way. Then, I apologized to all my family and friends, co-workers and everyone who were there to support me.

I wished I could turn back the hands of time. Sometimes, we make the wrong decision that can cause a lot of hurt in just a split second and cause a lifetime of pain. I hope and pray that when God does set me free again, that next time I make a better split-second decision.

I turned to the crowd and said, "I prayed that God judges me according to my actions and I thank Him for taking control. I finally see how life can hit you with a curve ball. I'm sorry to the ones I hurt and to the ones I love but I would love for you all to forgive me for my sins and never forget who I really am as a person. Thank you."

I turned around back to face the judge. She began, "I'm very sorry Mr. Tucker. I believe that you are not a monster from the look of your support system, but the law is the law, and I cannot overturn what the lawmakers have written before my time. I really hope this time you serve makes you a more of a beautiful person. You are not the monster the public sees you as. So, I close out this court with this to be said, "May God be with you and you walk this path with that same beautiful smile on your face. God Bless you. May He be with you Mr. Tucker. This court is adjourned."

She banged her gavel, and it was over just like that. Everything taken away from me...my wife, my family, my house, my job, my friends. I even thought about the torment I put Troy and his family through. I messed up big time. The police and detectives were going to catch up with Charity. She was going to really pay for what she did. I even let my mother-in-law down.

My stomach started to turn. I could only see emptiness in me. Only if I would've told my wife what was going on with me, instead of trying to be so secretive; my wife probably would have understood. She would've probably told Charity a thing or two. See how she took it when I finally told her, she wasn't even mad.

I guess when you really love someone, you truly love to the point that you would hurt yourself before you hurt that person. That's me, I guess. From that very moment, that weekend came back to me in a flash of me at that gas station when Charity asked me could she please bum a ride back to her vehicle.

I had a choice right there, to say No! I'm sorry, I'm really in a hurry. My wife is waiting up for me, she probably would've waited for the next man and mess up his marriage. But she set it all up. She figured her husband was messing around on her so she would find out his secret mistress and get even.

Yeah, she got even alright. All the way even. I guess the two found out the meaning behind death do us part. Well, as for Nicole and me goes, she will always be in my heart as long as these life sentences last. I think for the very first time in my life, I finally felt like justice prevailed for someone.

Well, I'm going to start this sentence off after it's all said and done. Hopefully, someone, some couple, husband or wife will start taking their relationship or marriage more seriously. Start talking, sharing their thoughts, their days and experiences with one another, because if they don't know their spouse or significant other, like they think they do their lives can change in an instant. Try to know each other so you can be able to talk about anything, and not be in fear of hurting or losing him or her. I'm Tyrone Tucker, may God be with me and you readers. Amen.

THE END

CPSIA information can be obtained
at www.ICGtesting.com
Printed in the USA
BVHW031350150321
602550BV00001B/97